MW00650762

King Harbor

To Mark —
Mark —
Sail on —

Other Books by Bob Bitchin

<u>Non-Fiction</u>
Biker
Letters from the *Lost Soul*
The Sailing Life

<u>Fiction</u>
(The Treb Lincoln Series)
Brotherhood of Outlaws
Emerald Bay
King Harbor

King Harbor

Bob Bitchin

FTW
Publishing, Inc.
www.seafaring.com

King Harbor

First published 2007 by
FTW Publishing, Inc.
Box 668
Redondo Beach, CA 90277
www.seafaring.com

Copyright 2002 by FTW Publishing, Inc.

All rights reserved, including the right to reproduce
this book and / or portions thereof in any form whatso-
ever.

This book is a work of fiction. Names,
characters, places and incidents are either
the product of the author's imagination,
or are used fictitiously. Any resemblance
to actual events, locals or persons,
living or dead, are entirely coincidental.

Printed and manufactured in
the United States of America.
First edition. June 2007
Cover artwork by Bob Bitchin

ISBN: 978-0-9662182-5-1

If you purchase this book without a cover, you should
be aware that this book is stolen property. It was reported as "unsold and destroyed" to the publisher, and
neither the publisher or author has received and pay-
ment for the "unstripped book."

$14.95

This book is dedicated to my wife Jody.
Thanks for putting up with me all these years.

Special Thanks

I want to thank my editor and friend, Sue Morgan, for editing the story and helping make it a lot easier to read. The fact that she has been a live-aboard sailor for over twenty years has, I am sure, helped bring into reality some of the sailing.

I also want to thank my brother, Dr. Alan H. Lipkin, for helping with much of the scientific jargon, and for helping develop something we hope will never be made in reality.

And most of all I want to thank my wife, Jody, who has helped me find the time to actually put into print an idea I have been working on for many years.

Chapter 1

As I climbed aboard *Lost Soul* I remembered why I hate boats! No matter how you baby and pamper them, they never seem to get enough of your attention. They just seem to find ways to remind you that they are the important one in the relationship. When I was younger I often wondered why it was they were referred to as she. After a few years of living aboard and crossing a few oceans, I started to understand the similarities. Like a woman, they seem to get jealous if you spend any time with another boat, and if you don't come home just one night they will make your life miserable.

It was a typical King Harbor morning in

Southern California. The sun was shining, the seagulls were soaring overhead, and bikini clad cuties were rolling along on wheels on the road in front of the marina. After spending the previous couple weeks delivering a new Catalina 42 sloop up to the Bay area, I was real glad to be back where the sun shines. Four hundred miles uphill is never a good sail, but this delivery had gone pretty much as planned.

I was delivering a new Catalina 42 from Marina Del Rey up to San Francisco for a broker I did a lot of deliveries for. After leaving Del Rey I sailed up past the Channel Islands in perfect weather. I sailed on a tight reach up to Point Dume, and then made a few tacks up past the Islands. I pulled into the Cojo anchorage and sat there waiting for a good weather report to make it around Point Conception. I timed my arrival at Point Conception for just before dawn, when the northeast tradewinds were the lowest, and once around that notorious landmark I'd just hugged the coast for the rest of the voyage. It's a long stretch of beautiful coastline as you make your way up, sailing past Big Sur and Monterey. It's beautiful, but dangerous, and with absolutely no place to pull in if you hit any trouble. It's about as rugged as a coastline can be.

I found myself enjoying the trip, watching as I paralleled Highway One. In my previous life, when I was riding motorcycles, this was my favorite getaway; throw a sleeping bag on the bike and ride up Highway One. It doesn't get any better, and I relived a few of the trips as I sailed passed Lime Kiln Cove and Big Sur.

After dropping off the boat at the dock in San Francisco, I picked up my paycheck from the broker who'd hired me to deliver the boat and grabbed a taxi to the airport. I couldn't wait to get back home. Of course, on my return, my baby made it known to me that I had better stop staying out for weeks at a time. Being left by herself, she always seems to get a real attitude. The longer we've been together, the more attention she wants when I neglect her. After this voyage up north, she was particularly displeased with me.

"My baby" is my home, a 56-foot stays'l ketch I named *Lost Soul.* I'd saved her from the bottom when she was about to be scrapped. After she'd gone around the world a couple times she'd been abandoned for a few years, and was in pretty sad shape when I found her. Since her shape pretty much matched my bank account, it seemed we were destined for each other.

At that time she'd been named Fairweather, but as soon as I saw her I knew she was *Lost Soul.* The name fit her, and it fit me as well. We were both *Lost Soul*s. It was pretty much the way I lived. In the ensuing years she won my heart. I worked hard to bring her back to the shape she should be in, and in turn she took me to the far corners of the earth, and she did it in real style. After almost 15 years we had put about 100,000 miles of blue water under us, and we'd seen the world.

We'd been home in the Portofino Marina almost a year, and since my return I had made a pretty good living at delivering boats, teaching sailing to new boat owners, and doing a little diving on the side. I found working for myself about the only way I could get through life. The biggest drawback to working for yourself is you have an asshole for a boss, but I felt I could live with that, as it beat the alternatives. It was a great life, and after spending any time cruising you come to realize that's what really matters - the quality of life.

As I climbed aboard *Lost Soul* on my return from 'Frisco I was greeted by a loud, obnoxious electric beep. In other words, my baby was screaming at me. The particular beep that was sounding meant either we were about to hit another vessel, or my bilge alarm was going off. Considering we were sitting in our slip, it told me my bilge pump was going off. Normally that would be a sign things were working well, but as I walked up to the boat I hadn't seen any water coming out of the bilge. That's not a good thing. The second thing I noticed was the "deep water" light flashing on the emergency panel. This was about as welcome as finding Charlie Manson at your teenage daughter's slumber party.

I lifted the floorboards hoping to find the pump switch had just stuck in the on position.

No such luck. There was black and slimy bilge water almost up to the floorboards, covering the fuel and water tanks. That pretty much meant we were sinking.

Oh boy. We were sinking. And in the slip, too. The folks in the marina would get a hell of a kick out of that.

I started to pump the emergency bilge by hand, which in turn started to bring the water down. That was a good sign. It meant we were not taking water on too fast. When I'd pumped enough to feel safe, I pulled my electric bilge pump up from the slime that gathered in the deepest part of the bilge. It was covered with the gook that always formed down there. It was a blend of fresh water, salt water, topped with a little diesel fuel, a few pints of whatever wine had been spilled on the floor over the past few years, and dust that filters down through the floor boards. Even though it was covered with slime, it seemed to be working fine. It was pumping its little heart out, but not taking the water down. As I was hanging almost upside down in the bilge, I looked over at the starboard bulkhead where the hose from the bilge exited the boat through a thru-hull. There I saw a waterfall that looked like a black and slimy Niagara Falls. It was pretty obvious there was a problem where the hose from the bilge exited the boat. My first five minutes on board and I had to fix something. Oh joy! Once again I was reminded of why boats were referred to as women. Go away for a little while and they will do just about anything to get your attention.

To access the particular area of the hull where the new Niagara Falls was taking place, I first had to move copious amounts of canned food that had been sitting in the starboard lockers since some long past voyage. Most of these had taken root by becoming rusted to the shelves. As I pulled these rusted cans away I realized that I had bought most of these stores when in Pago Pago, American Samoa, almost seven years earlier. It had been that long since I'd sailed in that area of the world. As I moved the cans from the shelf, I thought maybe I should try to rectify that lack of cruising sooner than later.

As soon as I had the rusted cans out of the way I pulled out the shelves, which gave me access to the bottom of the cabinet. I found the finger hole, and lifted the shelf out of the way. Then I found the culprit. Two, not one, but two hose clamps had rusted through, and the hose from the bilge pump had come off the through-hull. Instead of pumping the water out the through the opening in the hull, it was puking it all over the inside of the boat, and it cascaded down the bulkhead right back to the bilge. I wondered just how long I'd been aerating the bilge water. I jammed the hose back in place and Mickey Moused a piece of wire around the hose to hold it in place while I drained the bilge. Naturally, I had loaned my last spare hose clamp to someone on the dock awhile back and forgot who. I am sure they forgot as well. That was kind of how things worked on the docks. You need, you borrow. You have something another boat needs, you loan it to 'em. With any luck they even return it someday! Supply and demand.

Once the water level was back to normal I located the source of the original intruding waters. My packing gland on the prop shaft had loosened up on my last day-sail, and I didn't tighten it before I left. I could almost hear *Lost Soul* groaning in joy as I tightened it down and made her watertight once again.

I knew I was home. How did I know? Because it was time to head down to the chandlery and give them a bunch of money. That's pretty much a way of life for a boater. The best labor saving device for a boat would be a machine that printed out thousand dollar bills and automatically sent them to the various chandleries. It would save a whole lot of time and trouble. I still needed a couple hose clamps to make the repair a little more permanent, and I figured I'd get a few extras as backup as well.

After assuring my baby I was only leaving for a while, and that was to get some stuff for her, I left. I swear I heard her sigh as I walked away, or was it a giggle?

I walked down the dock a little way and ran into Sluggo. As usual he was elbow deep in seawater, packing slugs to be shipped to strange places so mad scientist could do God only knows what with them. He's a marine biologist, which sounds all fine and normal until you see what he does for a living. He goes out in a small boat, maybe two or three days a week, and picks up "squishies and squigglies." These he packs in large Styrofoam boxes, which he packs with ice to slow the little dudes' life cycles for shipping. He then overnights them to university laboratories around the world. Then mad scientists pull them out, torture them, and we are all assured that in some way this will eventually cure the common cold, or some such madness. But since slugs are ugly, to date there have been no "Save Our Slug" campaigns. It seems that people only picket for "cute" things. You know, "Save the Dolphin," mass murder the tuna. Slaughter the cow, but don't shoot Bambi.

Everybody kinda envied Sluggo. He had one of those lives you dream about. His work week would go kinda like this: On Monday, it's too early in the week to go out and get slugs, so he hangs out around the docks, giving advice to boaters who are doing various repair jobs on their boats. Tuesday he might be talked into going to the chandlery (kinda like I was talking him into now!) or find some other form of recreational activity. One week he took out the girls from Victoria's Secret for a photo shoot on his boat. Another week it was taking out one of the starlets from Baywatch for a special on "Sexy Swimsuits." We don't know how he kept getting these gigs, but he did. Usually it was around Wednesday, which he referred to as Hump Day, when he'd go out to collect sea slugs, his little one-footed friends. Thursdays it "didn't look right" and Fridays, well, it's too close to the weekend to work, right?

I sat on a dock box while Sluggo finished packing his squishies and squigglies. He was going to drop them off at UPS, and it was on the way to the marine store, where I had to go anyway.

"Got a new boat in over on B Dock," he told me. "Nice one, too. Musta cost a bundle. Even has one of those new satellite communication domes."

"Must be nice," I commented. A satellite communications system was on my wish list, but was going for over four and the airtime alone cost about the same as the payments on a small car.

"Uh huh," he grunted, and I sat in silence watching as he sent his next batch of squigglies to their various destinations to make mad scientists happy.

Across the channel something attracted my eye. It was the sensuous swaying of a great set of buns in a tight two-piece. I have always prided myself in the fact that I never missed much in that department. As I watched I realized there was a familiar rhythm to the swaying. I let my gaze rise a bit, and saw it was Mia. Mia and my old friend Dick Bondano had been dating for a while, and I wondered what she was doing over on B Dock. I watched as she walked up to the new boat that had come in. It was a Moody 64 with the name Julia II painted across the boom. Although it looked like it had seen some sea time, it was still a very good looking vessel.

As Mia started to board the boat I turned to Sluggo. "Hey, Sluggo, who's on the new boat that came in? I see Mia must know them."

Just as he opened his mouth to speak, the whole world erupted.

It was all in slow motion. The Julia II seemed to raise almost three feet where it sat, as a brilliant flash ripped it apart at the center. Mia had just set foot on the cap rail, and she was blown up and back almost 30 feet, over the boat in the next slip and hitting on the edge of the dock, bouncing into the water in the slip that sat empty. The sound of the explosion started as a rumble and expanded into a deep, thundering, ear-filling blast, followed shortly by a shock wave.

All of a sudden it seemed as if time was moving again. Sluggo and I both jumped up at the same time and hit the water. He literally lived in the water, and pulled away from me like Flipper leaving a turtle behind. By the time I reached where Mia had landed in the channel, he was already diving down to find her. I took a deep breath and started to dive to aid in the search. As I descended I tried to see through the murky marina waters. While I went down, I pinched my nose to equalize the pressure in my eardrums and tried to get deeper. The visibility was less than three feet, just about to the end of my arm. I was underwater for about 30 seconds, still trying to adjust to the bad visibility, when I saw a blur just below me. I could barely make out the form of Sluggo coming to the surface, and he had something in his arms. It was Mia.

As they broke the surface I could see she was bleeding from her scalp and she was not moving. Sluggo looked around to get his bearings, and started to stroke towards the nearest dock doing a one-armed backstroke and holding Mia firmly to his chest, with her head out of the water. I swam along side, wanting to help, but not knowing how. We brought her over to an empty slip on A Dock as gently as we could, and by the time we were there Scott and Pete were there to help us get her up. Scott was the marina manager and Pete was the local yacht broker. Scott got hold of her legs, while Pete grabbed her arms. Sluggo and I were in the water beneath her, so we just kinda pushed in the middle to try and keep her in a prone position so we could get her up onto the dock. Getting a body onto a dock is a lot harder than most folks think, especially when it's unconscious. It's kind of like trying to push a 125-pound sack of potatoes that didn't want to go.

Once she was on the dock Pete took off his shirt and bunched it up, putting it under her head as a pillow. Scott took off his shirt and started to tear it up, and as Sluggo and I got out of the water, he started trying to bandage some of the bleeding.

By the time we had Mia's bleeding stopped as much as could be done there on the dock, the Harbor Patrol showed up. They were over at the end of the dock, pumping water onto the flames which were enveloping the hulk that was once a beautiful yacht.

Mia was breathing, but barely. She was bleeding from the ears and nose, and was still out to the world. We all tried very hard to be patient waiting for the ambulance, as Mia's life seemed to hang on by a thread. Sluggo said he'd go with the ambulance and stay with Mia. That made the job of telling Dick what had happened fall into my lap. Since we'd been friends for over 20 years, I guess I was the best qualified, but I sure didn't feel as if I were. He and Mia were very close, and I knew this would be tough.

Chapter 2

The Kali Academy was located in a rundown area of South Los Angeles on Vermont near the 405 Freeway. It was a mostly commercial area with a lot of large, sprawling, older buildings. The building that housed the academy and its surroundings were clean and well cared for. Dick was the owner. He had started it as a school to help pass on the Jeet Kun Do style of martial arts, the teachings of Bruce Lee. When Dick was a youngster he had lived martial arts, and that love of a lifestyle had carried on well into his adult years.

I pulled my Harley into the parking lot and parked next to Dick's Panhead. We'd been riding together as long as I could remember, but I figure my memory wasn't the best, as I had lived through the '60s, and you know what they say, "If you remember the '60s you weren't there!" I was there, and so was Dick.

I walked in the front door and looked around. The walls were lined on one side by speed bags, and on the other by heavy bags. Assorted students were kicking and hitting the bags. Along the far wall was a mirror so students could watch their form as they worked out, and on the wall closest to the door was the sign-in counter. I walked over and an advanced student nodded toward the workout room. I'd seen him around, and he knew Dick and I were friends.

"Dick's giving a new guy some 'instruction' in the back room," he said, smiling. That meant he was letting one of the newbies see why being old didn't mean being slow, at least not in this business.

When I walked into the workout room, Dick was in the ring with a young student. The guy looked like he might be a gang banger, with baggy pants that hung down well past his knees, and a sloppy shirt that paid homage to some hip-hop group. He had a little sneer on his face. I knew that sneer would soon be gone.

There were about 15 people standing around the ring watching as Dick gave some close instruction to the student. Dick looked like a man of 35, even though he was looking at the backside of 50. His Hawaiian ancestry stood him well. No matter how many times I watched him in action, I always found it hard to believe that he wasn't a youngster. His speed was absolutely blinding, but his touch was as light as a butterfly. He would show a student a new move, and then keep increasing his speed until the student began to realize that someday he could do the same. When he would give an exhibition you had to tape it and play it back in slow motion in order to see all the moves. His speed was amazing.

He smiled when he saw me and gave me a wave of his glove. After a few more words of instruction he signaled to one of his assistants. A tall black youngster with some gang tattoos stepped into the ring. Dick whispered something to him and he nodded, then Dick left the ring. He walked over to me and we embraced. It had been awhile since I'd seen him.

"Let's go to the office and have a Coke," he said, and started toward the back room. "When did you get back from the City by the Gays?"

I followed him and tried to figure how to tell him about Mia. As we stepped into the office I decided there was just one way. Straight.

"I got back a couple hours ago." This was going to be tough. I knew he liked Mia a lot. "Dick, there was an explosion a little while ago at the marina."

"Oh?" He looked up, concerned. "Is *Lost Soul* alright?" It was just like him to worry about me first.

"Uh, yeah, she's fine, but it was another boat. A new one that had pulled in across from me."

All of a sudden he looked very worried. "Was Ronnie hurt?"

Ronnie? Who was Ronnie? I didn't know any Ronnie. He must have been confused.

"I don't know a Ronnie, but Mia was just going aboard when it exploded."

Dick stopped what he was doing and turned around. "Mia?" He looked at me like he didn't understand.

"She's on her way to the hospital. Sluggo went with her."

He turned and walked toward the door. Almost as an afterthought, he turned and looked at me.

"Well, are you coming?"

As he unlocked his bike and threaded the chain out from the wheels, I explained what had happened. Once the chain was off he straddled his bike and kicked the starter. After all these years he still refused to go with an electric start. He'd give it one slow kick to turn the motor over, and then another to feed the fuel. Then a hard kick to make it roar to life. It had been his ritual for years. The fishtail pipes let out a no-nonsense roar, and he let out the clutch and headed out of the driveway. We turned out of the parking lot and headed to the freeway on-ramp. We both accelerated hard as we entered the freeway and headed to the fast lane.

It was only a couple miles to Harbor General

Hospital, and it just took a few minutes. We pulled off the freeway and whipped into the lot. Finding a spot in the emergency parking area, we locked the bikes together and went to the emergency waiting room. Sluggo was there, and we walked over to where he sat.

"How's she doing?" Dick asked. "Any news?"

"Not yet. She was unconscious the whole trip here in the ambulance, and as soon as we got here they took her into that room," he indicated the emergency room, "and she's been in there since."

Dick started to walk to the door. Sluggo called after him. "Dick, you can't go in there. They're operating!"

It did no good. Dick walked to the door and pushed it open. In a matter of seconds he was being pushed back into the waiting room by a large male nurse and a doctor.

"If you don't sit down and wait I won't be able to finish treating her," said the doctor. "Now either sit there and be quiet or I'll have to call security!"

The next half hour went by very slowly. No one said anything, as there wasn't much to say, but little things kept going through my head. Things like, how did this happen? And why Mia? And last of all, who was this "Ronnie" that Dick had been so worried about? I would have to ask him about it, but this didn't seem to be the time.

In what seemed to be an eternity, but was probably more like an hour, the doctor came out wearing green scrubs. There were a few small spots of blood on it. His name tag said he was Doctor Ostriker.

"Who belongs to the girl in there?" he asked the group of us.

Dick stood up and walked over to him. "We all do, how is she?"

"Well, let's put it this way, we won't need a next of kin. She should be okay in a couple weeks. The explosion knocked her out, and that probably saved her life. She was unconscious when she hit the water. You guys got there fast enough to keep her from drowning, and the coolness of the water stopped the progression of some of the burns she suffered. If she'd landed on land she would be in a lot worse shape. As it is, a few bruises, a little concussion we have to watch, and some second degree burns." He stopped and thought for a second, then added as an afterthought, "Oh, she also broke a couple of ribs."

"Can we see her?" Dick asked.

"No, she'll be out for a few hours. We need to watch the concussion for a little while. She's under heavy sedation and is going to need a lot of rest. Probably best if you let her rest until tomorrow morning." Just then the door opened and a nurse rolled out a dolly. It was Mia. Her eyes were closed, and she looked as if she were sleeping. If it weren't for her swollen face and the numerous cuts on it, you would have thought she was just asleep. There were two bottles hung upside-down on a rack attached to the bed with tubes running into both of her arms.

Dick walked over and touched her hand, looking down at her. We could all see how this was affecting him. He just patted her arm and turned to me, nodding.

We thanked the doctor and headed down to the bikes. We were all anxious to get back and see what caused the explosion. Sluggo jumped on behind me, and we rode the five miles to the harbor in silence.

Chapter 3
. . . .

It was murky as I descended into the cool waters of the marina. The madness of the past few days seemed to move farther and farther away the deeper I went. The bottom was only 20 feet down, but it seemed as if it were miles away from the bedlam above. The quiet blanket of cool green water seemed to cover everything. The visibility was a little better now that the water had settled. It also helped that the sun was high in the sky and it was a clear day, kind of like people back East think it is all the time in Southern California.

I pulled myself down by grabbing what were once the lifelines of "Julia II," and drifted down over the starboard side. There didn't seem to be any damage there, and I slowly worked my way to the stern looking for anything unusual. There was nothing. As I worked my way around the stern I could see the dock lines where they had broken when the boat sank. There was nothing unusual here, either. I felt, rather than saw, motion above me and looked up. Dick and Sluggo were on their way down.

Since I was the only marine surveyor in the area that was also a certified diver, I had been hired by the insurance company to assess the boat's condition, to see if it could be salvaged. The first thing I did was to hire Dick & Sluggo as assistants. Might as well put the three of us on the payroll, and at the same time maybe we could find out what had caused all this. The Sheriff's divers had said it looked like a propane explosion, but something just didn't sit right. Dick's friend Ron had not returned to the boat and no one seemed to know where he'd gone. No one suspected him of anything, but it was awfully suspicious, and they really wanted to talk to him.

I worked my way along the port side of the boat and came to where the explosion had taken place. The fiberglass hull had been blown apart like a piece of wet tissue. The explosion had been centered right at the waterline. This seemed a little odd if it were a propane explosion. The propane tanks were located near the stern in the lazarette. The police said it was a pocket of propane that must have collected near the waterline, but that just didn't seem to be the case.

I worked my way awkwardly down the companionway, and Dick came down behind me. We swam down in the darkness using our Pelican underwater lights to illuminate the area of the explosion. The hole was a little over 18 inches in diameter, and was jagged and roughly circular in shape. It could be patched and the boat floated with the right equipment.

I shot a couple of photos of the damaged area, but the murky water made it tough. We slowly worked our way out of the boat, swimming around to the exterior of the side the explosion blew out, and took a few more photos. Then we headed to the surface.

"I think it's salvageable," Sluggo said. "All we have to do is cut a patch for the holed area, rent some air bags from Bobby & Billy over at Dive & Surf, and float her." I knew once she was afloat we could tow her over to King Harbor Marine Center to be hauled out, where we could do the salvage work. He made a very difficult job sound easy, but it looked like it could be done all right. Once on the dock we stripped off our wetsuits and adjourned to the "Yacht Club" for a little "warmth."

Latitudes & Attitudes is a typical marina bar. It's located over the coffee shop, with a great view of the marina. Everyone who has a boat in the marina just calls it the Yacht Club, because it's kinda like a private club. Since it's part of a large hotel and resort, the prices are, uh, shall we say "a tad high?" But the management, in their infinite wisdom, decided that anyone silly enough to be paying rent for a hole in the water should get a discount for drinking there. With our marina discount the prices were normal for a Southern California beach bar, just a little high instead of outrageous.

As you enter, the bar runs along the wall on the right with a large window behind. There is a scattering of tables, both low and high, with all windows overlooking the marina itself. A long mirrored wall runs the full length of the left wall, with the exception of the door to the restaurant. This makes you look at boats wherever you sit. If you like boats it's great. If not, well, what the hell are you doing at a marina bar?

Eric Stone sat on a bar stool tucked back in a corner by the fireplace playing with himself. Well, okay, so maybe I should clear that up. He was playing his guitar, accompanied by an iPod. He would sit at home and record all the sound tracks himself, playing all the instruments, then blend it together on his computer, and accompany himself when he would play at the bar. He looked up as we entered and nodded with a small smile. He was part of the extended family of the marina. The place was empty, as usual.

Eva was behind the bar. Even before we sat down she had glasses lined up and was pouring our "regular." That'd be an extra-large Captain Morgan's & OJ for me, a cold MGD for Sluggo and a virgin Bloody Mary for Dick.

"I have to submit the survey first," I said to no one in particular, "but I'm sure they'll total it. We should be able to pick it up for a couple hundred dollars from the insurance company after that, as long as the owner doesn't claim it."

"I just don't understand where he disappeared to," Dick said. "It doesn't make any sense. He really loved that boat and put everything into it. It's just not like him to disappear."

Sluggo and I had heard the story over the past few days as to where Dick and Ronnie knew each other. It was in Viet Nam, back when they were in Special Forces. They had both trained together after meeting at the induction center. Dick was Hawaiian and Ronnie a mix of Philippino and Dutch. Ronnie's nickname had been Snake. He was kinda small and wiry, and had hard blue eyes which always seemed to be laughing. He'd had a sense of humor that was very dry, and they had hit it off from the very start.

Eva brought the drinks to the table and leaned against my chair. I put my hand on her hip, and she bent over and gave me a kiss.

"So what did you find?" she asked. Eva and I had been dating for a couple of years. She loved sailing and was great crew. Besides that, she was built like a brick shithouse, always a plus in any boy-girl relationship. I'd helped her resolve a problem a few years earlier.

"Looks like something blew out the hull at the waterline," I said. "It sure doesn't look like a propane explosion. The propane locker is at the aft, and this was amidships."

"Oh, it wasn't a propane explosion," Dick chimed in, "it was set to explode."

He seemed awfully sure of that statement. Sluggo and I gave him our full attention.

"What makes you say that?" I asked.

He reached into his pocket and pulled out a small metal object. "This," he said, laying it on the table.

I picked it up and looked at it - a small circular clip attached to what looked like a safety pin.

"What is it?" Sluggo and I asked in unison.

"This looks like part of the triggering device on a placement mine. We used things like this back in Nam when we would have to disable VC trucks and things. Usually they are magnetic, so you just slapped them on the side of a truck or something, and then all you would have to do is sit back and within three or four thousand feet you could set it off with the flick of a switch."

"So you think someone not only blew up the boat, but did it knowing Mia would be blown off it?" Sluggo asked. "Why would anyone do that?"

"I don't know, but I plan on finding out," Dick said, and he picked up his Virgin Mary and took a sip.

"Count me in bro," I said

He looked at me for a second, and then he smiled. "I already did."

Chapter 4

Ronnie Tess slid quietly into the cool green water. He adjusted his facemask, bit on his mouthpiece and took a deep breath, testing the draw of air. It was just right. He dropped to the murky bottom and looked at his compass. He was almost a half-mile from where his boat had gone down, and he had to make it there and back without surfacing. He had parked his rental car near the horseshoe shaped pier and walked over to an area where there were a bunch of people getting ready to enter the ocean for a beach dive. It was a group of people trying to get certified to dive. The folks from Dive &

Surf were giving instruction on how to correctly enter from a beach when scuba diving.

He hung to the edge of the group and went unnoticed. Once he was in the water he swam off in the direction of the marina entrance, judging the distance as best he could. After a few minutes he located the bottom of the rocks that marked the breakwater at the entrance to basin B. He turned into the channel and started working his way further into the marina. He located the rocks that marked the channel's east side and swam along them, turning in and swimming under the fuel dock. He could see the fuel hoses from under the docks, and in a minute he was under the slips that held all the boats.

He turned to his right, staying just above the muddy bottom, and made his way to where Julia II had been berthed. He'd really loved that boat, and the thought of it lying on the bottom filled him with a burning desire to find out who was responsible for this. He had an idea, but wanted to know more. He'd found out about Mia being aboard when it happened, and that made him even more upset.

He and Dick had shared a lot of exciting times back in "the time" when they were fighting and playing in Viet Nam and Cambodia. When he'd sailed in and contacted Dick, it was just like they had never been apart. Dick's girlfriend Mia was the third Musketeer. They'd become real close in a very short period. It was hard to imagine it had just been two weeks since he'd first sailed into King Harbor.

He saw the wreckage of his boat lying just in front of him. Slowly he approached the boat. Just as he was about to swim over to the companionway he heard a splash come from above him. He ducked behind one of the concrete pilings and watched. The murkiness of the water helped hide him from view.

He recognized Dick as soon as he hit the water. There was also a big guy who came into view first. He didn't look familiar to Ronnie, but he was sure it had to be Dick's friend Treb. They had talked a lot in the past couple weeks, and it was obvious Dick and Treb were best of friends. He'd been due back a couple days ago. This had to be him. The third party in the water was Sluggo. He was the guy who'd been working on his ketch, Saga, the last couple weeks, across the way from the Julia II's slip.

Ronnie watched as the three of them swam around the boat. He felt his air start to draw a little hard and looked at his pressure gauge. It was less than 100 pounds. He was about out of air on his first tank. He reached behind him and pulled the cord to close off tank one and open tank two. He had coupled two aluminum 80s together so he would have plenty of breathing time on the bottom. He still had to get into the boat, grab what he'd come for, and get back out to the beach where he'd entered the water. He had about another 30 minutes, and if he could keep his breathing shallow he might make it. He drifted about a foot off the bottom, hiding behind the piling, hoping they wouldn't stay down long.

After a very long ten minutes they surfaced. He waited until he saw their shadows move down the dock, and then made his way to the boat. He swam down the companionway into the murky darkness. He made his way down past the engine room and into the aft cabin. It was hard to orient himself. The mattress was floating up on the ceiling and there was junk everywhere. He swam over to the drawers and pulled on the middle one. It was stuck fast.

"Yeah," he though to himself, "of course it's stuck. The wood's all swollen from being under water." He pulled his abalone knife that was strapped to his leg, and began to pry. Slowly the drawer came out. He pushed it away, and it floated to the ceiling, with all the other floating junk.

Ronnie replaced his knife and reached his hand into the hole the drawer had come out of. He reached in as far as his arm would go, and then began searching the backside of the panel. It just took a couple seconds. Soon his fingers made contact with a small metal box. He tugged at it with a hard jerk and it came loose. It had been held to the backside of the interior of the cabinet with a large piece of Velcro. As he pulled it out he saw that it had opened. One of the bottles had fallen out. He made a quick search with his hand and couldn't find it.

He figured the chances were it had opened during the explosion. He pulled his dive light out and looked into the deep and dark opening. He couldn't see it, and his time was running out. He put the drawer back in place.

He stopped for a second, thinking, and then reached in the same area, just a little lower. This time he pulled out a small canvas bag. It contained his custom .45 automatic. It was in a canvas case, wrapped in a gun cloth, and then put in a Ziploc baggy to keep the moisture out. He hoped it was watertight. This was his favorite pistol which he'd had built for him over 20 years ago. An AMT Hardballer frame, with a custom ramped action and a Colt barrel. It could fire both semi-automatic and automatic, and it was so well blueprinted it had almost no recoil.

He looked down at his pressure gauge. His air was getting low. He made his way back to the companionway and pulled himself up through the opening. Then he started his slow and easy strokes, to conserve air, and headed back the way he'd come. His mission had been successful.

Chapter 5

The Long Beach Saloon was a very upscale beach establishment when it was first built back in 1928. The well-to-do businessmen from Los Angeles would bring their wives down to the shore for weekends, and the Saloon was well known for their fine fare and comfortable atmosphere.

Even through the '30s and prohibition, the Saloon had prospered under the watchful eye of well-paid officers of the law who would make sure the fine clientele were not bothered by any silly rules against drinking. After all, a glass of fine wine was just that; fine wine, not demon rum.

During the '40s and the war years the Saloon prospered once again. The ship yards of Long Beach paid well, and the workers were always looking for a little escape from the every day world.

It was during the '50s that the place started to really deteriorate. The neighborhood went downhill, and the slide had not stopped. As the new century approached the old place just kind of gave up. Most of the small shops that surrounded it were empty, and the shoppers now drove to the WalMart Supercenter or the Long Beach Mall. Downtown was left for the hookers and the winos. The Saloon sat where she had been for 75 years, and she looked her age.

The interior of the Saloon had also aged. She was no longer the bright and friendly atmosphere that used to fill her tables. Now there was a bare neon bulb burning over the mirror behind the bar, and a small incandescent light glowing in the hall that led to the bathrooms and the back door. A pool table sat in the middle of what once was the dance floor, and an old hanging lamp advertising Bush Bavarian Beer glowed above the torn felt table.

Jim Pizzaro had lived in places like this since he was 18 years old, from the waterfronts of Bridgeport to the palm-lined streets of Long Beach. It was dark and quiet, just the way he liked it. Even though this was the first time he'd ever been in this particular joint, it was like home to him. The smell of old, stale beer and bar soap wafted through the still air. He didn't see a difference. It may be a different climate, but inside, the same; a beer-stained bar, a pool table that takes quarters to operate and usually has a rip or two in the felt, low lights to hide the old, frazzled barstools and seedy booths. It was comfortable; like home to him.

He was sitting at a table well covered by the darkness of the room, feeling very at ease as the front door opened and a ray of light surrounded a man as he entered the bar. Jim knew the man's eyes would be adjusting to the dark, so he took this moment to scrutinize the newcomer. Hispanic, about 35-40 and dressed like he was new to the country. This was probably the man he'd been waiting for. He watched as the new man walked over to the bar.

In a heavy Central American accent he asked for a cold Tecate with a lime. This would be Ramon. They had never met in person, but had talked over the phone, and they had set up this meeting almost a month earlier. The recognition signal was "Tecate with lime."

"This is fuckin' America," the bartender said when asked for Tecate. "We got Coors or Budweiser, what'll it be?"

"Hey," Jim said to the bartender. "Don't fuck with the guy, he's a friend of mine. Just give him a Coors and leave us alone. Don't get such a fuckin' attitude."

The bartender did as he was instructed. People

didn't tend to underestimate Jim. He wasn't all that large, about 5' 7" and 165 pounds when soaking wet, but his demeanor and long ZZ Top beard, along with the way he carried himself, made people think twice before going against him. Maybe it was the way he'd sit there in the darkened room with his wraparound sunglasses on that unnerved people.

Ramon walked over to Jim and held out his hand. "Mucho gusto," the man said in his native tongue.

Jim got up and walked farther back in the dark recesses of the room, putting his beer on a greasy tabletop and sliding into the red naugahide booth. Ramon followed suit and sat opposite him.

"Yeah, so is it done?" Jim asked. He had already verified that the job was completed.

"Si. No problemo. You have the rest of my dinero?"

Jim reached into his jacket pocket and handed him a rumpled envelope.

"This is what we agreed on. We're there any problems?

Ramon took a long swig from his beer and reached for the envelope. "No, senior. Everything was as you said." He hesitated. "There was a seniorita. She was on the boat, but other than that, the boat now sits on the bottom, as you directed." Ramon opened the envelope and looked inside. He pulled a few hundred-dollar bills from the center and was satisfied it was the agreed on $20,000.

Jim stood. "Good. Thanks. You going back to Mexico now?" he asked. He didn't really care, but felt like he should say something.

"Si, como no?" and with that he stood. "If you have further need of my services, you know how to contact me."

Ramon picked up his beer, chugged it down, turned and walked to the door, never looking back. He opened the door and walked into the warm California sun. After his eye's adjusted to the brightness he walked over to his brand new Ford F350 Lariat. It was the best money could buy. A dream truck which, if he were in Mexico, would be just that, a dream! A four-door crew cab with tandem wheels on the back and a Ford turbo-diesel engine that would pull stumps if it had to. Ramon felt bad for the Gringa that'd been hurt in the explosion, but the thought of how he'd be treated when he and this truck returned to his little village just outside of Monterey, Mexico, made it all seem to fade. In just one week he'd earned enough to put his family on easy street for the rest of their lives. It was like a dream.

He walked over to the pickup and pressed his hand-held alarm/lock remote. He heard the faint click as the doors unlocked. He opened the door and sat in the cool leather seats, running his hand over the cool smoothness. He turned the key and started to reach for the air conditioning adjustment... but he never made it. The truck exploded, much as the boat had exploded a week earlier.

As people gathered around the smoking ruins of the truck, no one seemed to notice the small man with the ZZ Top beard and hair as he left the bar.

Chapter 6

I could feel the boat move in her slip. I think that's one of the reasons I like living on a boat, the motion when you are just sitting aboard and relaxing. Landlubbers had to do things like cut grass and clean the driveway; I had to clean the growth off the bottom and varnish the topsides. It was a tradeoff I enjoyed. It'd been a few months since I'd laid on any varnish, and the wood was starting to show a little less shine than I like. Besides, I kinda look at varnishing as therapy. It's a mindless activity that allows one to think while you are working.

I'd already taken off the rubstrakes from the

starboard rail. I took a piece of 220 fine grit sandpiper and started to lightly scuff the surface of the beautiful teak. It would take about an hour of mindless sanding to prep the surface for a coat of varnish. That meant an hour to let my mind wander. I only did one rail at a time. If I did more than that it'd be like work instead of therapy.

It was obvious that the explosion on the boat had been inward. That pretty much eliminated a propane explosion. If it had been propane it would have happened at the lowest point of the boat, because propane is heavier than air. That was one thing. The other was, you could see the fiberglass had been blown into the boat, not out. That meant the source of the explosion was from the outside in. The little piece of metal we'd found told us the bomb had been set, and it was a booby-trap bomb. So someone had set it with the intention of sinking Julia II. All we had to figure out was the reason.

I found a small crack in the varnish and sanded a little harder until it couldn't be seen. I felt the dock under my feet start to bounce a little and looked down the docks. Dick and Sluggo were talking as they made their way down the dock.

"How's Mia doing?" I asked, as they got within earshot.

Dick picked up a piece of sandpaper and started sanding an area that needed it.

"Doctor say's she should be released in

another week. The concussion wasn't as bad as they thought. She had her towel in the bag she was carrying, and the explosion blew it up against her head, protecting her a little." He hesitated, and then went on. "It probably saved her life."

Sluggo had perched on the dock box. "Hey, ya missed a spot."

I called Sluggo my "tormentor" because he got a lot of enjoyment by tormenting me. He knew how to do a near perfect job at about anything on the boat, and would never miss a chance to point out a better way to do things, kind of like a mentor...only to an extreme. I'm the kind of guy that likes to get things done. I didn't mind having a bump or two in the varnish, but he'd torment me until it was perfect. With his "help" I usually ended up doing a much better job than I would have if I'd been left alone.

"So Dick, you never did tell me what Ronnie was doing here." I took a rag and wiped down the area I had just sanded. Was he working, or what?"

Dick absentmindedly continued to sand while we talked. "He never really said. He just glossed over it. I got the idea it had to do with something he found on his last cruise. He just got back from cruising the Line Islands south of Hawaii."

We worked in silence for a while, both thinking about what this might all mean, and Sluggo sat on the dock box pointing out our "holidays" which were the areas we missed with our brush, or covered too lightly.

Pete came down the dock and sat next to Sluggo on the dock box. "I just got a call from Abe over at the yard. He told me to tell you guys it would take about a day for the water to drain out of it, and then they'd have it on stands so you can check it out."

We thanked him, and made plans to meet him upstairs at the bar as soon as we finished the prep for the varnish. It turned out to take less than a half-hour, and we were all seated around two tables that had been pulled together in the bar.

Eric was setting up his sound equipment over in the corner, and Scott closed the marina office on the first level and came up to join us as well. This was pretty well a common practice at the marina. Sometimes it "just didn't look right" to work, and everybody would soon be up at the bar discussing whatever was the topic of the day. The yacht brokerage and the marina office were right next to each other on the dock, downstairs from the bar, and both doors had handwritten signs saying "Be Back Soon..." with a phone number. The phone numbers were their cell phones. If there was something important, they would be called.

Eva brought over a tray full of beer and we all grabbed one off the tray. "Cheers" said Pete, holding up his glass, and everybody chimed in.

A cell phone started ringing under the table

and six people pulled their phones out to see if it was theirs. I won (or lost?) the contest. It was mine. It was Abe at the boatyard.

"Hey Treb," he started, "you might want to get over here."

"Why, what's up? I thought Pete said you didn't want us over there until tomorrow?

"Yeah, well that was before our man Carlos tapped a drain hole into the hull to help it drain." He hesitated. "We found him out cold on the ground with the drill still running. You better get over here."

"Okay, I'll be right over." I hung up.

"Hey Dick, Sluggo, let's take a dinghy ride over to the yard. Abe says Carlos was knocked out by something that drained from the boat when he drilled a hole."

We tossed our beers down, and headed back to *Lost Soul* to get the dinghy.

The yard was in the next bay, about a 1/4 mile away. We could have walked it, but after awhile living on a boat you get to where, whenever possible, you take a dinghy. It made you feel like you were boating. It's a small pleasure, but a pleasure none the less.

As we pulled up to the dock, Sluggo tied the painter to a cleat and we walked up the ramp. We noticed a group of people standing around under the Julia II. Water was draining from the gaping hole in its side, and from a couple of other small holes. An ambulance was pulling out of the yard with its siren going.

"I called the police," Abe said. "I'm not sure what it is, but I've got a bad feeling, and I don't want any trouble here."

"You did the right thing. Thanks," I said. "How's Carlos?" Abe was the owner of the yard, and he was also long retired from the L.A.P.D.

"Carlos is dead. Died instantly. In all my years on the force, I never saw anything like this," he said. "One minute he was drilling some drain holes, and the next minute he dropped to the ground, dead."

I stood there for a few seconds, not knowing what to say. Carlos had worked for Abe for over 15 years, and I knew they were like family.

"Which hole was he drilling when it happened?" I asked.

He stood back from the boat pointing at a drilled hole just below the waterline on the port side. "It looked like that one. At least that's the one he was under. And look at this," he went on. "It looks like some kind of chalky residue where the water ran out of it. At first I thought it might be drugs, but it's not dissolving, which cocaine or speed would do." He rubbed his fingers on his chin, thinking. "This stuff doesn't dissolve. I figured you might know what it is."

I looked over at Dick. "Dick, do you think your friend was running drugs?"

He walked over and looked closer at the white residue. "No, I've known Ronnie a long time, and I know how much he hated what drugs did to people. He lost a few friends to drugs in his life, and he was pretty adamant about it. This has got to be something else."

He took out his Buck knife and stuck the end of it into the hole. When he pulled it out there was a small piece of glass stuck in the gook that was oozing out of the hole.

"Okay," I said. "Let's see if we can get it analyzed. Get some and put it in some kind of container, and hurry. Once the cops get here they might not look kindly on taking any of it."

Sluggo tore a piece of plastic off a drop cloth under a boat that was being painted and brought it over. Dick took a rag and wiped the white chalky residue on a small piece of it, being careful not to touch it, and jammed it into the container. Just as we got it wrapped up and tucked into our pocket a police car pulled into the yard.

Officer Landon Phillips was the first out of the car. He walked over to the gathering.

"Okay, what's going on here?" he asked.

Everybody kind of stepped back except for Abe. He had worked with Landon's father when he'd been on the force. Abe explained what had happened.

"Who belongs to the boat?" he asked, looking at those assembled as if they were all guilty of felony existing.

No one said a thing. Then Abe explained about the explosion, and how it was being hauled to be checked out. As they talked, Dick, Sluggo and I worked our way around the crowd and back to the dinghy. Fifteen minutes later we were back at the bar, enjoying a couple cold ones.

Chapter 7

Mia was starting to feel a little better. When she'd first come to she didn't know where she was, and her head hurt like hell. That had been a week ago. She sat staring at the tray in front of her, and was thinking that she'd much rather be sitting at the Yacht Club eating one of their great Wedge salads than trying to force down this soggy macaroni and cheese crap. She pushed the plate away and was reaching for the Jell-O when Dick and I walked in.

"Okay, when are you guys gonna break me outta here?" she asked. "The food here sucks!"

She reached up to Dick and gave him a kiss, and then me.

"I don't know," Dick replied. I'm kinda getting used to spending my nights with the Lakers Cheerleaders.

"Yeah, right! Like you could handle more than one woman a month!" Mia said, pushing him away laughing.

I sat in one of the uncomfortable hospital room chairs as Dick planted himself on the edge of Mia's bed. Dr. Ostriker walked in holding a clipboard. "Okay Mia, I guess we've done just about everything we can for you. I'm going to release you today. That work for you?"

Mia smiled broadly. "Yeah, It looks like I'd better get home so I can protect my property. I can be outta here in five minutes."

With that she whipped off the covers and stood up. Except for a small swelling under her eye and the bandaging on her ribs, she looked okay. She turned and walked into the small bathroom. As she turned she flipped the back of her hospital gown open where it was split in the middle and wiggled her bare butt in Dicks face. "Lakers Cheerleaders? Oh yeah? They got anything like this?" And she strutted into the bathroom.

Dick's eye followed her, as did mine and even the doctor's. "Dick old pal, I think you may be in for a little trouble the next few days!"

Dick turned to Dr. Ostriker. "Hey Doc, everything going to be okay?"

The Doctor looked at Dick. "Yeah, the concussion has subsided, and the cuts are all superficial. She'll have to keep the ribs bandaged for a few more weeks, but they are healing up fine."

"Thanks," said Dick. "I appreciate what you've done for her."

"Just doing my job," Ostriker replied. "Have you found anything out about the explosion yet?"

Dick reached into his leather riding vest pocket and pulled out a small plastic baggy. "Hey Doc, how would I go about getting something tested to see what it is? We found this residue on the hull of the boat that blew up, and need to know what it is."

Dr. Ostriker took the small container from Dick and looked at it.

"You can't tell by looking at it. I can send it to a lab to be tested. It might take a week or so. But I gotta tell you, if it's anything illegal they will have to notify the authorities, and they will tell them where it came from."

"That's okay with me," Dick replied, "but I really need to know ASAP. Any way to rush it up a bit?"

"Let me see what I can do. Give me a call tomorrow." And with that he turned and left the room.

"Hey Treb," Dick said. "We can't take Mia home on the back of our bikes. I'm going to head out and get my truck. You hang with her here for a little bit?"

"Sure Bro," I answered. "Go ahead. When you get back I gotta run down to the boat and take care of some business anyway."

A couple minutes after Dick left Mia came out from the bathroom. She was dressed in the clothes Dick had brought her the day before, and even managed to put a little makeup on.

"Where's my wayward angel?" she asked, looking around the room.

"He has gone to procure your chariot for the ride home. He didn't figure a ride on the back of his rigid framed bike would be the best thing for your ribs. Probably a good thing, huh?"

"Yeah, I guess. Have you found out anymore about what happened to Ronnie? It's really strange that he just disappeared like that. I'm really worried that something has happened to him."

I had been checking into things on his own, as I knew Dick was too close to Ronnie to suspect anything. I had gone to an old friend, Bob Fox, who was retired and living over on Catalina Island. Bob was ex-CIA before he became the Sheriff over in Avalon. He'd retired from that job a few years earlier, and was enjoying just being retired in a small town on a small island.

When Dick and I first met Mia she was a deputy sheriff in Avalon, working for Bob Fox. They had almost a father-daughter relationship, and she knew I would have gone over to talk with him.

"No, we haven't heard anything from Bob yet. I'm thinking about sailing over to the island this weekend to see him. You think you'll be able to take the trip?"

She looked at me with a grin. "You just try and keep me off that boat. I've been thinking a lot about what was going on, and I hope Bob can shed some light on what's been happening."

She walked back into the bathroom with her purse and continued to work on her face, trying to cover up any evidence of the beating she'd taken in the explosion.

Meanwhile, I went over in my head what they'd found out so far. I'd talked with Bob Fox the day before and what he'd found out was pretty disturbing. I hadn't even told Dick, because I didn't know how he'd take it. It was obvious he and Ronnie had been pretty close. I figured it might be better if he heard straight from Bob.

Dick only had to ride back to the studio to get his truck, and was gone less than 20 minutes. When he returned Mia was putting the finishing touches on her face, and walked back into the room.

"Okay big boy," she said, looking at Dick, "take me home and have your way with me.

Dick smiled at her. "Maybe we should wait until your rib's heal before we get into anything serious. I'm liable to crack a couple from the inside it's been so long!"

"I know you're bragging now," she countered

smiling. "After those cheerleaders, I figure you couldn't get it up with a six-pack of Viagra."

We walked to the nurse's station as Mia was rolled out in a wheelchair. It was the rules of the hospital. After a few minutes filling out forms and signing papers, she was rolled to the back door and loaded into Dick's truck.

"I'll see you guys later," I said, unlocking my bike. "I don't think I wanna be around for the next few hours watching you guys bump uglies."

I straddled the bike and hit the starter button, listening to the sound of the shotgun pipes as they started the slow idle that all Harley riders love to hear.

"Don't worry," Mia smiled, "he's only good for a few minutes anyway."

Dick slapped her on the butt as she slid into the seat. "Yeah, but it'll be the best couple of minutes of your life!"

Chapter 8

"Okay, cast off the stern line," I shouted at Dick and then looked forward, shouting at Eva, "Cast of the bow lines!"

They both hustled to the boarding steps and jumped on the boat as I put *Lost Soul* into reverse to pull out of the slip. As the boat started moving, the wind on the starboard beam started to push the bow to port. I whipped the wheel to port as well, to try and get steerage.

As the boat slowly backed out and gained speed, we started to get steerage and the boat responded to my touch. I loved the feel of *Lost Soul*. We had sailed so many miles together we were like one once we were underway. She'd been built over 25 years ago and we'd put over 100,000 under her keel together. We were pretty much made for each other.

As the bow cleared the pilings I put the wheel full to port and put her in forward, pressing the throttle. It stopped our backward motion and started to throw the bow to port. As soon as we'd come to a stop I once again threw her into reverse, pushing the throttle down. The prop always pulled to starboard. In this way I started to turn her and do a 180-degree turn in her own length so I could motor out of the channel.

The day was perfect for a sail. There wasn't much in this world that I could say I enjoy as much as taking off on a voyage with my best friends. Even if it was only the 30-mile-sail to Avalon, it was still an adventure.

Whenever you leave the dock, you never know what will happen while "out there," but it's always something. Every trip, even after all these years, brought me something new.

As we hit the main channel I made a hard turn to port, turning us into the wind. Dick was standing by the mainsail halyard and started to pull her up. In the meantime Mia and Eva started hauling up the mizzen. I kept her pointed into the wind as we traveled up the channel and released the mainsail sheet so she'd run free. Once the sails were up and the halyards tied off I cleated the mainsail and mizzen halyards.

At the end of the channel I turned her once again to port, to head out of the breakwater.

Now the wind was coming off our starboard beam, so I released the headsail furling line and started to pull out the sheet. The Harken self-furling gear started to spin, and the sail popped out and I swear I heard it scream, "I'm free!" I doubt that there is a better feeling on earth than the feel of a well-found boat healing over with the first puff of wind in her sails. It feels as if the boat just comes alive!

As we cleared the breakwater I checked the GPS and found our course for the R-10 buoy just off of Palos Verde Point. It was tight onto the wind, and we cranked all the sails in until they were as tight as we could get them. We were running at about 35° off the wind, and as *Lost Soul* hit the first swells she seemed to come alive. We started pounding into the swells and I hit the engine's kill switch, putting us fully under the power of the wind.

Eva and Mia headed down below to fix some sandwiches, and I turned the autopilot on and set it for the R-10 buoy some four miles ahead. There were no obstructions, and very little other boat traffic as it was a weekday, and most California sailors only go out on sunny Sundays.

I walked back to the aft deck-box where Dick was sitting and plopped my butt into a beanbag on the deck. Over the years I had learned that there is nothing better on a boat for pure comfort then the old 1960's style beanbags. Throw them anywhere on a boat and no matter how healed over you are it's comfortable.

"Dick," I started, "I gotta ask ya something about your friend Ronnie. I've been avoiding it, because I know you are old friends, but there is something I found out awhile ago, and I just didn't know how to approach it"

"Hey Bro, you know there's nothing I'd hold back from you. We've been through way too much together. Ronnie and I were tight in Nam, but that was too many years ago." He turned to look at me, "and besides, I think I know what it is you're going to say."

"Well, here it is. The police ran a check on Ronald Tess, and it seems he never came back from Viet Nam." I stopped, watching his face, waiting for a response. He just sat there looking at me.

"Dick, you hear what I'm saying? He was killed in Viet Nam. They say he was murdered while in a Viet Cong prison camp. He was listed as MIA for almost five years. Then, just after the "police action" was ended and we pulled out, his remains were sent back and he was buried in Arlington Cemetery."

Dick sat there. Then he said, "I lost track of him in Viet Nam. We were dropped on a mission. He never came out. He was killed." He stopped, looking down at his feet.

"A few days later the CO called me into his office. They told me his body disappeared. I wanted to try to find him, but they sent me home right after that. I never saw or heard from him

again until he called me the day he sailed in on
Julia II.

I got up and reset the GPS for Avalon's
waypoint. As we cleared the point I turned her
30° to port and watched as the autopilot brought
her around to the right course. Then I turned
and looked at Dick... waiting.

"He told me that he'd been captured and held
as a P.O.W. for almost three years, and then he
was released. His memory was all whacked up
and it took him years until he was almost normal.
He stayed in Viet Nam for a while and then
worked his way by boat to the Gilbert Islands,
and then the Phoenix group, and ended up in
Fanning Island, near the equator. He ended up
working at a small dive shack."

I watched Dick's face and waited. I could see
he was trying to put this all together. "How'd
he get the boat? That's a pretty expensive thing
for somebody in the backwoods taking divers
out," I said.

"He told me an old guy pulled in about a year
ago to do some diving. They'd gone out to do a
"drift dive" at the entrance to the reef."

"Drift dive?" I asked.

"Yeah, they do it a lot on atolls. You boat out
to the entrance of a lagoon and drop into the
water. The current carries you through the pass
at 4-5 knots. All you do is drift and enjoy the
coral and fish. Anyway, he said he was holding
the dinghy while the old guy was drifting ahead
of him. As they drifted over the edge of the

lagoon there were a bunch of sharks hanging out. They do that to catch anything dead or injured that comes through the pass."

I tried to picture this in my head, and didn't like what was coming.

"Well, it seems this particular day the old guy was what the sharks found. Before Ronnie could get to him the sharks hit him. They hit him hard. By the time Ronnie got there and pulled him out he was pretty badly mauled. Ronnie took him back to the village Matai, or leader, who was the closest thing to a medic they had on this little island. For the next few days Ronnie did what he could to help the guy. They became very close after that." Dick sat back and thought for a minute. "At least that's what he told me." He seemed lost in thought for a second, and then he shook his head as if he was coming out of a dream. "I had no reason to doubt him."

Just about then the girls came up from down below with a plate full of sandwiches and a couple bags of chips.

"Don't worry," I said quietly to him, "we will get to the bottom of this." I hoped I wasn't lying about that.

The wind was starting to come around a little more off our beam, and it was starting to freshen. I eased the sails and pulled out the staysail as well. This was turning into a great sail.

As we hit the mid-channel buoy we started to cross the traffic lanes for the shipping that headed down the coast of California either for Long Beach or headed down further to the Panama Canal. There were only two vessels, one heading north and one south. It didn't look like we were on a collision course with either, so I adjusted our heading a little so we'd come into Descanso Bay, just a little west of Avalon.

There wasn't a lot of conversation for the next hour as we all enjoyed the sun and wind, and one of the best sails across the channel I could remember, a broad reach at seven to eight knots with an occasional nine showing on our knot meter. Very respectable for a "Taiwan Turkey," which is what a lot of boaters had nicknamed sailboats that were from that region of the world. That was because a lot of the early boats that were built there were full keel, heavy displacement sailboats that couldn't sail to weather very well. Over the years that had changed, but the nickname stuck.

As we approached Descanso Bay I went below and prepped the anchor locker. I had to make sure there were no obstructions that had fallen on the chain pile, which could hinder the free flow of the chain as we anchored. Descanso Bay was very deep, the shallowest anchorage being over 90 feet, and most of it was 120-130 feet deep. Most boaters pay for a mooring to avoid anchoring there because of the depth, but I have always preferred putting my own anchor down. Besides, I find dropping a hook and setting it easier than picking up a mooring, and

I trust my anchor and chain more than I trust a mooring that has been there God knows how long, and could be in bad condition.

I pulled into an open spot and started to let the chain out. We were in 90 feet so I let out the full 400 feet of chain. A little over four-to-one scope was okay for a protected anchorage like this. Usually I like to put out a minimum of five to one, but since all I had was 400 feet, that was what I put out.

Once the anchor was down I put her into reverse and pulled the chain out straight downwind. That should hold her from drifting unless the wind changed, which it seldom does in Descanso. Our rearward motion came to an abrupt halt, and I knew we'd set the hook good.

After few minutes we had launched my Apex inflatable and got the 30 horsepower Honda outboard fired up. We were soon working our way through the crowded anchorage of Avalon, heading for the dinghy dock.

Chapter 9

. . . .

Pizzaro watched the ketch *Lost Soul* as it pulled out of its slip. He sat in his hotel room in the Portofino and switched off the surveillance camera and shut off the phone tap. He couldn't monitor them while they were at sea with what he had setup there in the room, but he was still listening to the conversation between Treb and Dick via the bug he'd placed under the ledge of *Lost Soul*'s aft deck-box.

He'd checked into the hotel a week earlier after he'd followed them home from the hospital. As it turned out, it was a good thing Ramon had screwed up and blasted the girl. It gave Jim a person to track in his search for Ron

Tess.

Pizzaro had been tracking Tess across the Pacific and everywhere he went, but he'd lost him after the explosion. He had to find him, or he'd be in very big trouble with some very bad people. In the early years Pizzaro had been with the CIA for 10 years, and he got tired of getting the meaningless jobs while others were being promoted around him. He was disenchanted with his life with the Company, but had no other place to turn. Then some people had approached him. He didn't know who they were, but they knew an awful lot about him. As they say, they made him an offer he couldn't refuse.

He started doing small surveillance jobs for them. Simple things: follow a scientist for a month, check out some chemical company in France. Just a lot of little things, but the money was very good. Then one day they asked him to hit some guy. They didn't give him a reason, but said it was worth "big money." He agreed, found the mark and took him out. The next day $200,000 was wired to an account that had been set up for him in Zurich.

He'd found a home. He let the people know he was available for similar wet work if the pay was the same. After that he traveled all over the world. He stayed in the best hotels, hired the best call girls, but he still felt more at home in a seedy waterfront dive than anywhere else. It was almost two years before he found out that he was working for a very covert division of the

National Security Administration, the NSA.

As *Lost Soul* cruised slowly down the channel on its way out of King Harbor, he started moving. He knew he'd lose reception from the bug as soon as the boat was over a mile away, so he decided he'd better get over to Avalon on Catalina Island and see what he could find out. If he couldn't find Tess, maybe these guys could. They seemed to know him pretty well. And besides, it was his only lead.

He buzzed Robert down at the concierge desk and told him he needed a cab and a ticket to Avalon on the Catalina Express out of Long Beach. When he'd checked in he had tipped Robert pretty well. In his years with the CIA he knew there was nobody who knew more about what went on around a hotel than the concierge. Robert was no exception.

The Portofino was a marina as well as a hotel, and that was what made it ideal for him to watch these people. His room overlooked the parking lot and the marina, and gave him a direct view into Treb's boat.

He changed from his t-shirt and jeans into a sport shirt. He wanted to look like a tourist so he would blend in when he got to Avalon. No one knew him there, but you never knew when you'd have to disappear. He slipped on a pair of Teva sandals and headed for the stairs.

At the entrance to the lobby he found Robert talking with a couple of people. As soon as Robert saw him he tore himself away from the conversation and walked over. Pizzaro thought maybe he'd tipped him too much to make him that anxious.

"Mr. James," that was the name he'd check in under. "I got you a ticket on the 10 am Express. I already told Big Paul, the cabbie, how to get there, so you should make it in plenty of time." Robert stood there, waiting, knowing there would be at good tip in this for him.

Pizzaro peeled off a ten from his roll and handed it to the waiting man. "Did you get me a round trip ticket?" Pizzaro asked.

"Yes sir. I figured you'd want to come back. It's an open ticket, good for any of the return trips. I charged it to your room," Robert said, as he slipped the tenner into his pocket. "Have a good trip."

After he got settled in the cab he started thinking about any of the hundred things he might have overlooked. He knew that there was some way to get back on Ron's tail, but he just couldn't figure what he was missing.

"Going over for a little vacation?" the cabbie asked.

"No," Jim mumbled. "Just shut up and drive."

The cabbie went back to his driving. Pizzaro looked at the back of the man's head and then at his license that all cabs were required to post on their visor. He had long dark hair in a ponytail that was well into turning grey. He could see him in the rear view mirror watching him. He was wearing an old flannel shirt, kind of faded, and his arms were covered with tattoos. He was either an old biker or an ex-con. Maybe both. Pizzaro knew there was something wrong when he looked at the license. This guy was not Achmed Doorian, as the license stated. If he was, he'd put on a lot of weight and aged about 20 years. The license showed a clean-cut guy with short dark hair and no tattoos.

"Okay," Pizzaro asked, "what's your game?"

"Wadayamean 'game?'" the man asked.

"Well, first of all, the guy back at the hotel said your name was Big Paul, but your taxi license says Achmed Doorian, and unless you've had a pretty friggin rough last couple years, you ain't the guy in the picture."

They stared at each other in the rear view mirror, trying to read one another.

"Yeah, so what? You gonna turn me in?" Paul asked,

The man just looked annoyed.

"No, but it looks like you might ride," Pizzaro hesitated for a moment and then continued. "I might be looking for a little information about a couple local bikers. You know any?"

Paul studied him in the mirror, then asked, "You a cop, or what?"

"Pizzaro smiled. "No, I ain't no fuckin' cop. Just looking for someone, that's all. I can make it worth your while if you can help me."

Big Paul considered this for a moment.

"Yeah, I been riding around here for 30 years or so, but why'd I want to talk to a rude fucker like you?" He was still stinging from the "shut up and drive" thing.

Pizzaro pulled his wad out of his pocket and held it up so Big Paul could see it, saying, "I need some info, and I don't mind paying for it. Good info pays good. Bad info gets you hurt."

Paul looked at the wad and all of a sudden he could see there might be a light at the end of his troubled tunnel. Paul had lost his license a few weeks back because of a couple DUIs. Then he lost his apartment a week ago because he couldn't pay his rent. He'd been sleeping on his ex's couch for the past week, which was a real bitch as she'd married a very square citizen who looked at him like he had cooties whenever he saw him. He had to borrow a friend's taxi license, and the guy got 25% of whatever he made, so he just kept getting in deeper and deeper. He figured all he needed was a little starter money and he could get some crank. Once he had some crank he'd be okay. He just knew it.

"Okay, but how do I know you're not a cop. I ain't no snitch!"

Pizzaro said, "Don't worry about it. I'm just looking for a friend of mine. Guy about 5'6", maybe 165 pounds. He has Filipino features but very blue eyes."

Paul thought for a minute. It didn't sound like anybody he knew, but he wanted that money, so he figured he'd lead the guy on and see what he could get.

"Yeah, yeah. That sounds familiar. What's his name?"

"He wouldn't be using his real name. He was hanging out with a guy named Dick Bondano, rides an old Panhead. Brown with a dragon painted on the tank. Do you know him?" Pizzaro asked. Then he continued. "Also a guy named Treb Lincoln. Rides a black shovelhead with fat-Bob tanks and ape hangers. Big guy."

Paul thought for a second. "Yeah, I know this guy Treb. Big guy? Tattoos?"

"That sounds like him," Pizzaro responded. "What can you tell me about him?"

"That depends on what's in it for me," Paul said. "I ain't just gonna tell ya shit and then have you stiff me." With that he started to pull the cab over to the side of the road. He wanted to check this guy out before they went any farther. They'd just gotten off the Long Beach Freeway and were heading for the parking lot at the Catalina Express terminal.

He pulled to a curb and they got out of the cab and faced each other. Big Paul had gotten his nickname back before they were being facetious with nicknames. Nowadays they'd name him Tiny. He was living up to his name. He was about 6'3" and probably weighed in at around 225. He was wearing a Barnett Harley-Davidson t-shirt with the flannel shirt over it. He looked like he could take care of himself.

Of course, Pizzaro wasn't worried in the
least. In his hand was a Walther PPK 9mm
automatic. He kept it in a hip holster out of
sight, under his sport shirt.

Paul looked at him and could see something
in his face that made him give the man some
respect. Even though he was wearing dark
glasses, Big Paul could almost feel the tension.
Just as he was trying to decide if he should try
and mug this guy and take his wallet, Pizzaro
seemed to read his mind, and smiled.

"I don't think you want to try anything." He
watched as Paul got a confused look in his eyes.
Then he continued.

"Like I said, I'm not a cop. I'm just looking
for this guy, and he hangs with the people I just
told you about. It's that simple."

"Yeah, right," Paul said. "Like I'm gonna
take your word for it."

With that Pizzaro pulled the Walther from
behind his back and aimed it at the middle
of Paul's chest. He was very casual about
it, like they were discussing the weather or
something.

"A cop wouldn't pull a gun on you, would
he?" Pizzaro asked. "And if he did he wouldn't
just shoot your big ass, would he?"

Paul thought about the small .32 automatic
he had in his boot, but couldn't think how the
hell he could get to it. So instead, he just stood
there.

"So once again, with feeling now. Treb

Lincoln and Dick Bondano. What do you know about them? Be quiet and get shot, or speak and I'll make it worth your while."

"Okay. What the hell. Can't hurt." Paul thought for a second before continuing.

"Lincoln used to head up a group of bikers that were fighting the helmet laws. He and Bondano put on a big run about 15 years ago taking a shitload of bikers to Washington to protest the stupid lid law. He got in some shit with some druggies awhile back, and he kind of disappeared for a while. He showed up a few years ago on a boat and seemed to have changed his life. That's about all I know." Paul stopped, waiting to see if he'd get an opening.

Pizzaro thought for a minute. He knew all about the protest and the stuff that had gone down in Costa Rica with the druggies.

"I'm looking for something more recent." With that he tucked his free hand into his pocket and pulled out the wad of bills. Paul's eye's followed his hand, and Pizzaro knew what he needed to do. He stuffed the wad back into his pocket after he pulled the top two bills off. They were hundreds. He pulled 'em out and showed them to Big Paul.

"Now, for the $200 question." He could see Paul's mouth almost watering for the money. "If he was hiding someone, where would he hide them?"

Paul thought for a moment. He'd ridden with Treb back during the helmet law protest, and even worked with him trying to keep things organized. He didn't want to get him in trouble, but $200 worth of crank, if cut properly, would make him $500 or more on the streets.

"Well, he lives on his boat in the marina, but I've heard he has an apartment somewhere that not many people know about. Maybe I can find out for you?" He figured, why settle for a couple hundred now if he could milk this guy for more. He seemed to have a lot of money, and Paul knew the first rule of doing business like this; if you pull a gun, use it. This guy wasn't going to shoot him. If he was he'd have already done it.

Pizzaro considered what had been said. "Okay," he said. "Here's a couple hundred. After you drop me off at the Express office see what you can find out." He noticed the cell phone on the dash and added, "Give me your cell phone number and I'll call you in two days to see if you've earned any more."

Big Paul looked at him. He could see this guy meant business, and besides, he could use a little side money to get out of his current financial woes.

"Okay Boss, you got it." He pocketed the money and opened the door for Pizzaro. "I'll see what I can find out for you." With that said, he climbed back in behind the wheel, considered the gun in his boot and dismissed it just as fast.

They rode down the street in silence and pulled into the Express parking lot and Pizzaro got out of the cab.

"That'll be $22.50," Paul said.

"Yeah, right!" said Pizzaro as he turned and walked toward the Express without paying.

Chapter 10

Bob Fox was feeling old. He knew there was a good reason for that. After all, he'd lived a lot longer than he'd ever expected to. In three months he'd be turning 80... 80 years on this stupid planet. It didn't seem possible.

He sat on a stool at the Norm's Place, a little coffee shop that he liked down on the pier. It was home to him. He'd been the sheriff in this town for almost 20 years, and since he retired almost two years earlier he felt he knew the town better now than he had as sheriff.

"What do you think the weathers gonna do, Bob?"

It was Norm Quient. He and Norm had

been friends for more years than either of them wanted to admit to. Bob took a sip of his coffee and set the cup down.

It's funny, he thought. The older you get and the less time you have left, the more you enjoy taking your time. The clock ticked a couple of seconds off and he replied, "Probably the same thing it's done for the past two weeks. It'll be hazy until the sun burns through, and then we'll have another beautiful day. Those guys in the Chamber of Commerce will be straining trying to pat their own backs congratulating themselves for it."

Norm looked out into Avalon Harbor. It was filled with boats of all sizes and shapes. There were huge motor yachts with their old men and young women, and fishing boats filled with anxious men waiting to go out and "catch the big one."

Norm liked the sailboats best. He'd been a sailor all his life and still managed to get out once in awhile. He'd even convinced Bob to go out with him a few times.

"Now there's a nice boat," he said to Bob and pointed out to the eastern edge of Descanso.

Bob turned and looked. His eyes weren't as good as they once were, but for his age he still had pretty good vision at a distance. "Ah," he said to Norm. "Now you have good taste! That's *Lost Soul*. That's Treb's boat. I'll bet Mia and Dick are with him."

He slowly got up from his stool and pushed

a dollar bill to Norm, who was working behind the counter.

"Oh stuff it, ya old coot," Norm said. "I'm buying this one. Go see your friends." Norm and he had been playing that game longer than either could remember. Back when Bob was Sheriff Norm wouldn't let him pay for anything and he still wouldn't. It had a little to do with friendship and a lot to do with respect. Norm was one of the few people in Avalon that knew Bob Fox's past. There was no way he'd ever pay for anything is his establishment as long as he lived.

Bob slowly made his way down the dock that sits in the middle of the small crescent-shaped harbor known as Avalon, looking forward to seeing Mia again. Mia Albro had been a waitress at the local bar, it seemed like decades ago, and they became friends. One day he hired her in the sheriff's office which, at that time, was just a one-man office. She'd started as a clerk, just tidying up and taking care of the copious paperwork that was the bane of his existence. After awhile she started handling some calls. After one particularly harrowing experience with a couple of drunks, she decided to take a marshal arts class. It wasn't until about a year later that he'd met her instructor/boyfriend from the mainland, Dick Bondano. At the time they were into things a little deeper than they could handle, and Bob was able to help them out by approaching some people from his past.

For almost 30 years, long before he moved to Avalon to be Sheriff, he had been with the CIA. It seemed to him like it was another lifetime.

He watched as the dinghy was lowered from the davits on the back of the boat, and he could make out four people getting into it. As they got closer to the dinghy dock he recognized Eva and Treb, along with Mia and Dick. He couldn't help but smile. These were his favorite people in the whole world.

As soon as Mia saw him standing on the dock she started waving and a big smile was on her face. Even before the dinghy hit the dock she was standing up and seemed to be jumping up and down. She didn't even wait as the dinghy was being tied up. She ran up the ramp from the dock to the pier and wrapped her arms around Bob. They just stood there for a long moment, holding each other. Mia had tears in her eyes as she kissed him on the cheek, and he felt his heart swell.

Just then, Dick came up the ramp smiling. Mia reluctantly released her grip on Bob, and Dick gave him a hug. "How the hell are you, ya old fart?" Dick asked, with a big smile on his face.

"I'm gonna outlive your scrawny ass," Bob retorted, smiling.

Eva and Treb had finished tying up the dinghy and reached the top of the ramp. Once again Bob was taken by how beautiful Eva was. They had been friends for a few years, but her dark hair and blue eyes still gave him chills. She gave him a hug and a kiss, and he looked at Treb. He never seemed to change. They embraced and all five of them headed down the dock to Norm's Place.

"So Mia, how are you feeling? Everything healing up?" He asked. When she'd been hurt and he found out about it he was on the next shuttle to the mainland. She was more like a daughter to him than a friend, and he was more like a father to her.

"Yeah, everything seems to be working. I started working out again a few days ago. Still have a lot of stiffness, but it'll work out over time," She said.

Dick looked at her and then said, "She's turned into the terror of the gym! Ever since her accident she's been working out harder than ever. Some of the younger students are afraid to spar with her." He smiled, his face filling with pride.

"Well," Bob went on, "don't take it too hard. Muscles take time to repair." He hesitated, and then went on, "Did you ever find your friend Ron?" he asked, turning to Dick.

"No, and as a matter of fact, that was one of the reasons we sailed over. We wanted to see if maybe you could give us a little help," Dick said.

Bob replied, "If I can I will, but I've been out of action for a few of years. There's not many people still around I can ask a favor of."

"Here's the problem," Treb started. "It seems Dick's friend Ronnie Tess was reported killed in action in Viet Nam, and here he shows up on a yacht 30 years later, very much alive. He says that he'd been captured, and after the war he wandered around the Western Pacific islands and ended up on a little atoll called Fanning."

"So what can I do?" asked Bob.

"Well," continued Treb, "we were wondering if you might be able to check and see if the CIA has any information on Ron. He's been missing since the explosion and it's not like him. He seemed just like his old self back in Nam until this explosion, and then he just disappeared. One doesn't just disappear in Southern California."

Norm wandered over and said hello to everyone. He'd been listening down at the end of the counter. Wiping a glass with the bar towel as he talked, he said, "A lot of things can happen to a man in a prison camp. Maybe he did change. Maybe he had something to do with the explosion."

They all looked at him, and he could see that everyone dismissed the idea as soon as they thought about it.

"I went through hell with him while we were over there, and I know him. There is now way he's mixed up in anything clandestine." And with that said, Dick got up and walked over to the rail of the pier.

Mia got up and walked over to where he was standing. "You know, he could be right. He could have changed over all the years."

He turned and looked into her eyes. "No. There is no way. He and I spent a lifetime in the couple years we were in Nam. I knew him too well. It's not possible!" The look in his eyes told her just how sure he was of that.

She took his hands in hers and looked up at him. "Okay. Then let's find out what's going on and stop messing around." With that she turned and walked back over to where the rest of them sat.

"Okay," she said, in a voice that she hoped was commanding. "We will assume he is innocent. So we have to figure out just what it is that was going on that brought this all about." She hesitated, "So where do we start?"

Bob's training from his old days started to come back to him.

"Well," he said, "the first thing we have to find out is what the substance was you gave to that doctor to test. When are you supposed to know?"

"That's kind of weird," Treb answered. "Dr. Ostriker sent it to his lab to check out, and they said it was lost before they could test it. He pushed them and said they started to get very odd about it."

"Odd?" Bob asked. "How so?"

"Well," Treb went on, "they said at first it was very difficult to analyze, so they had sent it on to a government lab. It was there it disappeared."

Bob said, "I'll see if I can find anyone who

I can talk to. Meanwhile, how about we have dinner over at the Galleon. Mia, they'd love to see you again."

"Great," said Mia. "I'd really like to see some of the old faces as well. Let's go." She turned to Norm. "Hey, Norm, you gonna join us?"

He looked at the scattered people who had just come in on the Catalina Express. "No, I think I'll see if I can't make a dollar or two off the tourists. Things have been a little slow lately."

"Okay," Bob said. "I'll see you later," and the five of them walked off toward the Galleon. It was just about a block down the street that fronted the beach. It was usually tough to get in there when the tourists were packing the beaches, but this was a weekday and a little slow.

As they walked down the pier Norm noticed a man that had just gotten off the Express who seemed to be watching them with particular interest. Most tourists, when they arrived in Avalon, would stand and look out over the beautiful bay, or scan the hillsides that overlooked the bay. This particular guy seemed to have nothing but eyes for Bob and his companions. Norm kept an eye on him while he wiped down the counter. After a minute watching them enter the Galleon, the man walked over and took a stool at the counter.

"What can I get you?" Norm asked in his

most professional voice.

"You got a Budweiser back there?" the man asked and turned to look at Norm through questioning eyes.

"Coming right up. You just come in on the Express?" Norm asked.

"Yeah. I noticed you talking to that group that just went into that restaurant over there. Friends of yours?"

Norm didn't like the way he looked. Something wasn't right. He decided he'd better play it cool until he could find out what the man's interest was in Bob and his friends.

"No. They just sailed in on a sailboat. Had a beer and asked about a good restaurant. An old guy sitting here suggested the Galleon, and they went to check it out." He stopped. "You know them?"

"Oh, just thought I might recognize one of the guys. The big one. Did you hear his name?" the man asked Norm.

"No. Didn't catch it. Why don't you go ask him?" Norm smiled at him.

"No. Not important." He reached into his shirt pocket and pulled out a photo, showing it to Norm. "You ever see this guy?"

Now Norm knew he didn't like the guy. He treated people like they were just there for him. He took a long look at the photo, studying it, and then answered. "Doesn't look familiar. But we get a lot of people through here."

"Okay. Thanks," the man said, standing.

"What do I owe you for the beer?"

"Two bucks," Norm responded.

He watched as the man pulled a roll of hundreds out that would choke a horse. He unrolled it and there were a bunch of ones in the middle. A Kentucky bankroll is what they used to call that where Norm came from. Shysters and con men used to carry a roll like that.

As the man walked off toward the restaurant Norm picked up his phone and dialed Bob's cell phone.

When the group had arrived at the entrance to the Galleon they were greeted like the old friends they were. Toni and Patty, the two waitresses, were hugging Mia and they were all talking at once. This was something that Treb could never figure out: how women can sit around, all talking about different things, and actually communicate and understanding what's going on. He just shook his head and smiled.

Meanwhile Bob walked back to his favorite table and pulled out one of the comfortable captain's chairs. He sat down and watched his young friends and for the first time in a long time, actually missed his youth a little. Truth be told, he was glad he was getting old. So few men from his previous profession actually reached retirement age, much less lived to his ripe old age. He actually enjoyed the little aches and pains he got. They reminded him he was still here, after all these years. Watching these young people made him remember his younger days. Maybe he didn't miss them, but he had sure enjoyed them.

His cell phone starting to ring interrupted his reverie. He answered and listened for a couple seconds. Then he just said, "Thanks Norm. See you for coffee in the morning," and pressed the disconnect button.

He signaled to Treb, who was looking his way. Treb walked over and sat down. "Yeah Bob, what's up."

Bob explained the phone call from Norm. Treb thought about it for a couple seconds and started to get up. Bob stopped him with a hand on his arm.

"Wait a minute. This guy may have something to do with your friend being missing. Let's see what we can find out." With that he got up slowly and walked over to a table near the door. He stopped and looked out the window, trying to spot the man his friend Norm had described. It only took a second. He was sitting on one of the benches on the beach across the street. He was watching the door.

Bob walked slowly back to the kitchen. "Hey Patty, you got that Polaroid camera you use to shoot pictures of VIPs here at the restaurant?" He asked.

"Sure Bob, it's in that top drawer over there by the door."

"Thanks. I'll bring it right back."

He walked back over and got as close as

he could to the door. He knew because it was light outside and darker inside the guy probably couldn't see him. He snapped off a couple of shots. After he ripped the developing film out of the camera he took it back and stuck it in the drawer.

"Thanks Patty," he said. I'll get you a new roll of film later."

"Don't worry about it. You've done plenty for us. Did you see a cutie out there?"

"Yeah," he said. "A real cutie."

Bob walked over to Dick and Treb, who were sitting at the table now. He threw the photos on the table.

"You guys know him?" he asked.

They had all checked him out through the window. They'd never seen him before. They told Bob that.

"Okay. When Toni or Patty come by order me a small filet, medium, with a small salad. No potato, I have to watch my girlish figure," Bob laughed. "I'll be right back."

A minute or so later he was walking into the office he knew so well. It was his for years. It was the Sheriff's office. His replacement, Tom Cray, was sitting behind the old desk. His feet were up and he seemed to be fitting very well into the slow pace of Avalon.

"Hey Cray," Bob asked, "can I use the scanner and computer for a second? I want to check someone out."

Cray shook his head in the affirmative. "Sure

Bob, hell, I still feel like this is your office and I'm just baby-sitting it for you."

Fifteen minutes later Bob was back sitting at the table eating a great filet with just salad, no potatoes. It was a good feeling to be sitting with friends, enjoying the afternoon.

Chapter 11

Ron Tess was running out of options. Ever since Julia II had blown up he feared he'd been discovered, and he had to stay out of sight. He'd gotten his package out of the boat, but he knew there was a chance they might find the other bottle that had gotten lost in the hull. It was well hidden, but they might have found it. The first thing he did was to check into a cheap hotel on Pacific Coast Highway just a few blocks from the marina. He knew better than to check in himself, so when he saw a "working girl" on the street he made her an offer she couldn't refuse. All she had to do was check into a room for a week under any name she wanted, and he'd give her a hundred bucks. That way no one could identify him if they started a search. After she'd checked in he came to the room and sent her packing. Then he just kicked back and started thinking.

He felt very bad about what had happened to Mia. Seeing his old friend Dick Bondano after all those years had made him a little too comfortable, and he knew he must have been discovered, but for the life of him he didn't know how.

He thought back through the past few weeks and couldn't come up with the answer. All he knew was, the only man he had ever trusted in his life, Dick Bondano, now thought he was a crook, or worse.

When they had gone through Special Forces training before being sent to Viet Nam, they had hit it off like long lost brothers. The fact that Dick was Hawaiian and he was a combination of Filipino and Dutch had put them into some category the rest of the troops tried to keep segregated. It didn't bother either one of them. They had both been brought up in households that were steeped in martial arts, and they spent a lot of their off hours teaching each other their particular styles. Dick was better than anyone he'd ever met in Jeet Kun Do, and Ron was a natural at Tai Kwan Do and Judo. By the time they were sent in-country they were both experts in all three styles. That was probably what kept them alive so long.

Their particular skills made them invaluable to the Rangers. Once the were in-country a routine set in. That was about the only thing that kept them sane. They would give each man 10 South Vietnamese soldiers to train, a Squad. After a three-week training period they would be parachuted behind the Viet Cong lines. Then it was up to them to cause all the trouble they could cause and work their way back to their own lines.

It finally turned into a contest to see who could bring the most of their soldiers back alive. It was a tough way to go. Until the last parachute drop, Ron had been winning. He had one drop that he returned from with three men. The most Dick had made it back with was two.

Both of them had taken several rounds over the course of a very hectic year. They wore their wounds almost like a badge of courage, and would always joke with each other over whose exit hole was bigger.

The last time Dick had seen Ron they were being dropped farther back than they had ever been dropped. Ron and his team went first, then Dick's a few minutes later. They'd been dropped about 15 miles apart. They could communicate with their walkie-talkies, which had been reduced to a small earpiece in the helmet with a lapel mike. On Ron's last transmission all Dick heard was a lot of gunfire and heavy breathing. Then the mike went dead.

Thirty years later he got a phone call at his

martial arts school. Ron was nervous as long-tailed cat in a room full of rocking chairs as he waited for the phone to be answered. Then it was picked up.

"Kali Academy," a female voice said. "Can I help you?"

Ron was almost afraid to say anything. Then he muttered, "Is Dick Bondano there?"

The woman, who he later learned was Mia, told him to hold on for a second. In what seemed like an eternity, but was probably more like a minute, he heard the familiar voice on the other end of the line. All of a sudden it was like 30 years just passed in a moment.

"Hello, this is Dick," and he waited. "Hello," he said again after a few seconds, "is anyone there?"

Ron tried to talk, but found his throat was tighter than a wedding night pussy.

"Hey Mia," Ron heard over the phone. "You sure there was someone on this line?"

Ron finally worked his throat open, and croaked, "I'm alive!" He couldn't think of anything else to say. Thirty years and that was it. Meanwhile, Dick was starting to think it was a crank call.

"Well good for you," he said sarcastically over the phone. "So is your mama, and I'm busy!"

"Wait Dick, it's me! Ron Tess."

It had taken a few minutes to convince Dick it really was him. He'd called on his satellite phone from about 10 miles off the coast of Los Angeles. After telling him a little of his crossing Dick told him to pull into the Portofino and called his friend Sluggo, who lived on a boat down the dock from Treb, to see if he could talk to Scott about getting him a slip. It would take a couple of hours for him to sail in, and they were very long hours.

In the next two weeks they spent a lot of time together. The years melted away. Ron told Dick about how he was captured, and what he went through in that prison camp. It was hard to see who felt worse, Ron for having to tell him about it, or Dick, having to listen to what he had gone through.

"So when the war was over they didn't bother to tell us," Ron had told Dick. "I escaped after a couple years and made my way into Cambodia. It was there I heard the Americans had gone home. I felt betrayed, like they had forgotten me," he said.

Over the weeks he told Dick he had worked as a fisherman in Thailand and Cambodia. He'd been working on a boat that was going to head over to the Gilbert Islands. When he saw them he thought they were the most beautiful islands he'd ever seen. He said he decided to find an island somewhere and just hide from the world.

After a couple years he said he ended up on Fanning Island. That was it; the most beautiful island he had ever seen. He jumped ship there one night as his boat was pulling out. For days he just walked the beach, living on coconuts, papaya and mangos and an occasional fish he'd catch in a shallow spot. He thought he'd died and gone to heaven.

There were only about 900 hundred people on this little atoll in the middle of the Pacific. The few people that lived there were about as friendly as any he'd ever met. Most of them were originally from the Gilbert Islands.

He met a John Williams, a cruiser on a sailboat who was sailing through the islands, and helped him repair his boat when he hit the reef. Over a period of time they became friends. Ron took him out for a drift dive and saved the man from a shark attack. A few weeks later, as they sat there over a couple of lobsters that Ron had caught, the man offered Ron a deal he couldn't refuse. That night they set up a plan to have a dive business on this out-of-the-way paradise. He told Ron to get a hut built on the inner lagoon, and said he'd be back in about two months. He was going to sail up to Hawaii and get some dive gear and see if he couldn't get more cruisers to head this way. He wanted to share this paradise. Back then only about 8-10 cruisers a year would come through Fanning on their way to Samoa from Hawaii or Tahiti, or other points south.

It sounded good to Ron. He'd been certified as an instructor when he was in the Rangers, so it wouldn't be a problem. And so he built a small palm-frond hut and even put in a small pier. Two months later John Williams returned. He had six sets of tanks, a bunch of snorkels, fins and regulators, and a genuine Poseidon air compressor. He'd thought of everything. He even brought a dozen five-gallon cans of gas to run the compressor. They were in business.

Williams took off to finish his sail around the world, and Ron stayed there to "run the business." This consisted of being a beachcomber most of the time, and then, whenever a cruising boat would come in, he'd see if they wanted to do some diving. As he knew the reefs there better than even the natives, most of them would take him up on it.

The funny thing was, they'd give him money. He had no idea what to do with it. There were no stores on Fanning. No place to spend it. After about a year he did manage to spend a little buying gas from a boat that could spare it. Other than that it was just a pile of useless green stuff.

Dick listened over the weeks and tried to imagine all that had happened to him since those days long ago in Viet Nam. It was hard for him to imagine Ron's life on that distant island. It was also hard for Dick to understand how he'd ended up with Julia II. It was obviously a very expensive sailboat, not something you'd just pick up anywhere. When asked about it Ron would edge around the question, just saying that he'd gotten the boat after he left the island. He never really said why he had left his paradise.

He also never told him about the five years after he got out of the prison camp. There was no way he could tell even Dick about that, or about Milani.

Chapter 12
. . . .

Treb, Dick, and the girls had spent the whole night anchored in Avalon and they enjoyed it even more than they'd hoped for. Seeing Bob was always great, but the fact that they found the guy following them was a real bonus.

After they'd finished dinner that night, they'd walked Front Street for a while after Bob had gone to turn in. Mia wanted to go and see a couple of her friends who were still working on the island, so she and Dick took off. That left Eva and Treb to their own devices. It had been right there in Avalon, the first time they'd ever made love. It seemed just like it was yesterday at times, and other times it seemed like they had known each other forever.

They walked down the pier to the ramp that went down to the dinghy dock. It was a beautiful night. It was so clear you could see the lights of the mainland glittering from 25 miles across the Catalina Channel. As they went down the ramp and untied the dinghy Eva held onto his arm, and all of a sudden she grasped it tight. Treb turned to look at her and she was staring back up the ramp. At the top stood the man they had seen earlier.

"Don't worry honey," Treb assured her. "I'm here, and I can take care of you." He turned and started up the ramp, but she held him back.

"No. No. I don't like the looks of him. He's evil. I just know it. Let's just go out to the boat." And with that she hurriedly finished untying the dinghy. When Treb turned around to look back up the ramp, the man had gone.

Once back out on the boat they forgot all about him. In fact, they forgot about the whole world. In the two years they had been together the original feeling he got the first time he saw her was still deep within him. It wasn't so much her beauty, but what was inside. It just seemed to shine right from her soul. They spent awhile sitting on deck enjoying the evening and making love. Sometime after midnight they heard the shore boat pull along side and heard Mia and Dick climbing aboard.

The next day they went in to meet Norm and Bob for breakfast. Bob had been up and at 'em early. He said that lessons from life are hard forgotten. He'd been an early riser all his life, and couldn't see a reason to change just because he was retired.

At 7:00 am he was at the Sheriff's Office and on the phone. Sheriff Cray wouldn't be in until around 9:00, but Bob still had a key to the office and he figured it would be easier to get things done if he were alone. He started placing calls from his "little black book" and before long he had been put in touch with a man who'd worked with him when he was down in El Salvador back in the late '70s. The guy had been new to the company and Bob, who went under the name of Foxfire back then, was in charge of a covert operation that was supposed to help end the fighting in the country. Of course, it didn't do any good because the powers that be, in order to cover their asses, had put in a second team helping the other side. They figured that way no matter who won, they'd be on the winning side.

Of course the farmers and people of El Salvador were the only real losers. But when you're sitting in a big house in Fairfax County Virginia, you tend to forget the little people. That was why Bob had quit after all those years. His move to Avalon had no doubt saved his life.

In any case, he found that Val Strasser, who was the young recruit, had stayed with the company, and was now the ADDO (Assistant

Deputy Director, Operations) in the home office. With a job like that, Bob knew he'd be in the office on Saturday. That was one reason the company preferred single men. It wasn't possible to get ahead if you wanted a life as well.

Since Virginia was on Eastern Time, it was well after 10:00 am there. It took a few minutes to get through the tight security at the switchboard, but a few remembered names got him through to Strasser.

"Val," he started, "this is Bob Fox. Is your memory good enough to remember me?"

Val could almost feel the tight-lipped smile on the other end. The time he'd spent in the jungle with Fox had steeled him and readied him for a lot of what would come later. For Val Strasser, Bob Fox was "that teacher," the one you never forget.

"Hell yes, you old fart. What are you doing still alive? I figured they'd have buried you long ago," he said laughing.

"Naw. I'm way to ornery to die. You know what they say, 'Old spooks never die, and if they did you wouldn't know it.'"

"I heard you were in some hick town playing Sheriff," Val said. "You still doing it?"

"No," Bob replied. "It was in Avalon, on the island of Catalina, and it was the closest thing to heaven you could imagine. I retired a couple years ago," he hesitated for a second, and then continued. "Val, I have some young friends that seem to have gotten into the middle of something, and I'm trying to help them out. If I e-mail you a couple of photos could you run them for me and tell me what you come up with?"

Val thought for a second and realized how much he owed this man. "Yeah. No problem. I'll see what I can do. E-mail them to me and be sure to send 'em to my personal address, okay?" He gave Bob the address. It didn't take very long. The photos of Ron and the man outside the restaurant were in CIA headquarters in a matter of minutes.

Bob made a couple more calls and then left the office, locking the door behind him. He walked down the street, heading for Norm's Place on the pier. When he arrived Norm was pouring coffee for a lot of the regulars. Bob sat down at an empty table and Norm walked over with a cup filled with black coffee.

"Well," he said, "did you guys know the dude I called you about?"

"No," Bob said. "But we got a good picture of him and we should know something soon. Have you seen him again?"

"No. I think he knew I wasn't real fond of him. But this is a small town. If he's here we'll see him again. Count on it."

Just then he saw the group of Bob's friends coming up the ramp from the dinghy dock. They all walked over and pulled up chairs. They asked for coffee and Norm went off to get it. The girls went to help him.

"So anything new yet?" Treb asked Bob.

"No. But it shouldn't be too long," he answered.

The rest of their breakfast was filled with small talk. Just before they finished, Sheriff Tom Cray was walking down the dock. He walked up to the table and pulled up a chair.

"Coffee?" Norm asked from behind the counter.

Tom had never turned down cup of coffee in his life. Before he'd come over to Avalon as Sheriff he'd spent 30 years as a cop in Hermosa Beach, a small town across the channel that was known for its great beaches and nightlife. Most of his career he spent walking the beaches of Hermosa, sipping on a tall to-go cup of coffee, telling pretty young girls to put their tops back on, and dumping beer from people drinking on the beach. You might say it was perfect training for his new job.

After breakfast Bob and Sheriff Tom walked back to the office. Bob wanted to see if he'd gotten an answer yet. One thing about those guys in Virginia, they did things fast.

When they got back to the office Bob logged on at the computer on the second desk. Sure enough, he heard the "You've Got Mail" sound. He trashed a couple of spams and then opened the one from Strasser. As he read the note he realized they were into something bigger than they knew.

To: Bob Fox, Avalon, California.

From: Val Strasser, ADDO, Quantico, VA

Item#1 – Ron Tess. Last seen 10 years ago.
Captured in Viet Nam 1967. Escaped 1972.
Recruited by the Agency on his return. Death
certificate on file. Operated out of country
in S.E. Asia for five years. Excellent record.
Disappeared 10 years ago. No record since.

Item#2 – Jim Pizzaro. Recruited out of
the marines by the CIA at age 22. Fifteen years
service. Two reprimands (excessive violence)
and one suspension (theft of evidence). Left
the Agency of his own will five years ago. Is
said to be a covert operative for unknown
agency. Possible NSA. The NSA disavows any
knowledge of his existence.

Bob sat there and reread the e-mail. It was
sent in a "no print" document that was designed
by the CIA. He knew it would blank from the
screen in a minute or two so there would be no
record of it. One of his talents learned in the
old days was a very good memory. Even at 80,
that was still working.

He stood up staring at the now blank screen.

"What's up Bob? You look like you've seen
a ghost." Tom was once again seated with his
feet on the desk.

"Maybe something worse than a ghost." He
reached into his shirt pocket and pulled out the
photograph of the man they'd seen last night.
He took a felt tip marker out of the glass jar
filled with pens on Tom's desk and wrote "Jim

Pizzaro–NSA?" on the back of it.

Tom read what he wrote, even though it was upside down. "NSA?" he asked. "Is this guy supposed to be here in Avalon?

"I took this picture of him yesterday afternoon," Bob said. "Outside of the Galleon."

"Let me have that photo," Tom said. "I'll get some copies made and get them around the island. We sure don't need any of their shit going on over here."

In a few minutes Tom had put together a small information page with the photo on it. It told anyone who saw this person not to engage him in any way, but to call the Sheriff, and then he had put his phone number on it.

"I'll get these out right away. If he's still on this island we'll find him." Cray said.

Bob left and went to find Treb and Dick. He had to tell them just who it was they were dealing with.

As he expected, they were still sitting around the table on the pier in front of Norm's Place. As he approached them he tried to think of an easy way to break the news to Dick that his friend hadn't told him the whole truth.

It seemed the best way was right out, so he started with "Dick, Ron Tess was a CIA operative for five years after he escaped from the prison camp in Viet Nam. He served in Southeast Asia the whole time. He disappeared about 10 years ago. There is no other record of him."

He waited as that sunk in and then continued.

"The guy that we saw watching you last night? His name is Jim Pizzaro. He's also ex-CIA, but now it's possible he could be working for the NSA. He's an assassin."

No one said a word for almost a full minute.

"Well," Dick said," it could be worse. Ron could have been the bad guy." He tried to smile.

Bob looked at him with a sad face. "Maybe he is," was all he could say.

Once again, Silence.

Chapter 13

Dr. Albert Boredanski was not a very happy man. For a day that had started out so well it had turned completely sour, but at least it could not get any worse.

As a highly published organic chemist specializing in a group of natural occurring plant toxins known as alkaloids, he held a very cushy position at Grant Memorial University in the beautiful countryside of eastern Tennessee. He did research funded by the National Science Foundation. The NSF grant not only funded his research, but paid for a teaching assistant who taught all his classes.

Every once in a while he would give

a lecture to one of the classes. He enjoyed interacting with the students and found it a welcome break from working in the laboratory. He often chose the nursing classes just to intermingle with the students. He was greatly appreciated as an entertaining and charming lecturer and had often met and dated pretty coeds through his infrequent lectures.

Dr. Boredanski had a weakness for young girls. That was how he'd ended up doing additional, specific research at the request of the NSA. It began one afternoon after a class, when Bonnie Zyrnoff, a particularly attractive young lady, wanted to talk with him about the lecture on the very poisonous indole group of alkaloids. During the discussion in his office, Bonnie's extreme friendliness and extraordinary appearance were intoxicating. He had asked her out and in a week's time, Albert was hopelessly in love.

Not only was Bonnie beautiful, but it turned out that she had some very exotic tastes. She was bisexual and had shyly asked if she might bring her girlfriends along for some intimate sharing. Albert took to the new lifestyle eagerly and his tastes for the erotic grew and grew, until he was living for the weekends when the "girls" would come over and they would only take time out for meals.

After a few months, Bonnie and her friends showed up one evening with a strange man. At first the Doctor thought they had something new in mind. Although they did indeed have something new in mind, Dan Smithwick was also interested in plant toxins and had even had a particular research interest. Albert would do anything to continue living the life he had come to love and agreed to look at a problem that had been intriguing Smithwick for some time.

And so it was that the NSF grant had additional, and very generous, funding. Albert's lab was never lacking for modern equipment or the latest in chemical instrumentation.

Dr. Albert Boredanski had earned a reputation by creating a revolutionary new group of toxins derived from indole alkaloids. The concept involved substances that were extremely reactive. So much so that they were unstable and would oxidize fairly rapidly in the air. The presence of oxygen caused them to react, to form unusually toxic transient intermediates that only survived a few minutes prior to oxidizing further to harmless substances. The substances were synthesized under nitrogen gas and kept in evacuated glass vials. When introduced to the air in the presence of laboratory rats, it became instantaneously lethal and killed them in less then a minute. His new benefactors had learned of this, and wanted him to perfect it as a possible weapon or war. As a patriotic American, he had no qualms in helping his country, and the girls kept coming. He had everything he ever dreamed of and it only seemed to get better and better.

He was working on the timing of the reaction. The idea was to have the initial oxidation occur rapidly, forming the lethal toxin which would slowly continue to oxidize into harmless substances in a mater of minutes, so that soldiers could walk the battlefield after an attack without the bulky contamination suits.

He had achieved his goal. He had come up with a compound that was synthesized under nitrogen and could be subsequently stored in a vacuum in glass vials. When the content was exposed to even the smallest amount of oxygen it would become instantly fatal. Its activity would persist for about a minute as it was oxidized more slowly to a harmless substance. Once it was exposed to oxygen it would be active for less than a minute, becoming a smoky precipitate which would settle out as a fine, chalk-like powder.

That weekend the girls showed up right on time. They had been extremely enthusiastic and ingenuous with their lovemaking. By the end of the weekend Albert was exhausted. After they'd gone, he felt that he had conquered the world. He had bragged to Bonnie and the girls about the breakthrough he'd made earlier in the week and how he'd supplied Smithwick with a half dozen samples. He knew they would be glad for him. He told them that he had decided to name his new concoction Zyron, in honor of Bonnie Zyrnoff, the love of his life.

And that was why, sitting here the next

day, he was a very unhappy man. He was unhappy because he had just learned how little he had really meant to Bonnie and the girls. They'd been using him. It was now apparent that they didn't love him at all, and they were only playing him along so he would work for their boss at the NSA.

He learned this when, just now, they had stood outside his office with Dan Smithwick who was holding one of the evacuated vials. Smithwick was smiling as he threw the glass vial into the air and slammed the door very quickly. It landed with a loud pop as the vial imploded, spraying the now lethal toxin into the air. He heard the girls giggling as they walked away from his locked office. The last thing that went through Dr. Boredanski's mind was the fact that he would, indeed, never see his girls again.

Chapter 14

· ·

Ron Tess lay on the uncomfortable bed and listened to the sound of traffic outside. He was soon in the half sleep of a mind-weary man. He traveled back to where he was the happiest, and his dream lingered there.

He was back on Fanning Island. He had just surfaced and looked around for his client to do the same. He had taken a couple from New York for a dive. They had just been diving on an old oil tanker that had sunk in the lagoon 20 years earlier. It was a fairly easy dive; about 35 feet in crystal clear conditions. Mike and Sue Morgan were certified divers, so this was an easy gig. Just take them around and show them the sights.

They were sailing around the world and had arrived on Fanning on their 35- foot Cheoy Lee yawl named Because. Their last stop had been on Christmas Island after a 900-mile passage against the prevailing winds. They were planning to stay for a week, and had met Ron after the second day. Ron had just set up his dive shack, and these were his first customers.

When they surfaced they all climbed into the 12-foot Zodiak and got out of their dive gear. Only Sue had worn a wetsuit, as it was pretty warm water.

"Let's go back to the boat for lunch," Mike suggested.

Ron was famished. "You're on," He said.

On the way back to the boat all Ron could think about was how much he was loving his new life. The five years he'd spent in the CIA were behind him, and he was finally starting to relax. He knew he'd found the perfect life, and he was starting to settle into it.

On their arrival at the boat they were greeted by Milani. She was the daughter of Ione, one of the elders of the village. The Morgans had agreed to let her clean their boat in exchange for some supplies. That was a way of life on the less populated islands of the Central Pacific.

Ron hadn't really noticed Milani before. He'd been so intent on setting up his dive shop, and it was on a small atoll almost a mile from the major atoll where most of the people on

King Harbor

Fanning lived, he'd never noticed how attractive she was.

Milani was 24 years old, and she was still single. This was not the norm on small islands. Normally a woman was married by the time she was 17 or 18. Ron had wondered about that, but never asked.

As Sue prepared a lunch of canned peaches and fish sandwiches on home made bread, the four of them sat around the salon table and laughed about the dive and great time they'd been having. Ron had a hard time keeping his eyes off of Milani. He had never noticed how her eyes sparkled, and the rise and fall of her breast beneath the simple pareo kept making him lose his train of thought. None of this went unnoticed by Mike and Sue, or Milani either.

After lunch Ron stood to excuse himself, as he was feeling very self-conscious all of a sudden. He mumbled something about having something to do, and he was getting ready to dive in and swim to shore when Milani walked up to him and touched him on the shoulder. He felt a shock go through his body, straight to his soul.

"Would you mind if I swim in with you?" Milani was asking.

Ron didn't notice the look that Sue gave Mike, or the knowing nod he gave back.

"Err, uh, no, I mean yeah, sure!" All of a sudden Ron was more tongue-tied then he'd ever been in his life. He felt so nervous inside it was like he was back in the jungles of Viet Nam and was surrounded by the enemy. He didn't know what to do.

Ron's life had been very simple until that day. He'd joined the service when he was only 17, and even though he was not unattractive to women, he had been totally involved in martial arts all his life. Women never played a part.

Once he was in-country he had gone with "the guys" and partied with the girls in the bars and hotels that proliferated the towns where the soldiers would go for R&R. But the thought of a romance was out of the question. They were just whores. One didn't get to know whores. It wasn't done.

And so it was that here, on board the yawl Because, he had met his match, a 100-pound island girl by the name of Milani. He couldn't fight his way out of this feeling. He couldn't run away from it. He just hurt inside, and didn't know why.

They swam ashore together, and once on the beach she looked at him for a very long minute, smiled, and said simply, "Thank you," as she turned and walked off the beach.

For days the picture in his mind of her walking up the beach toward the village would not go away. He memorized every curve, every sway of her hips, and the way her wet pareo clung to her strong buttocks; the way the sun gleamed off her wet hair, and her tan back.

It was almost three days before he could go to sleep without seeing her standing there before him on the beach, and he'd relive the words "Thank you" over and over.

He started making excuses to go to the small area where Milani lived. Each time he would look for her, but she'd be gone, out washing clothes by the well, or gathering fruit on outlying motus.

He found himself turning back to his guerilla training. He started watching her movements as she'd go through her daily routine. And each day he realized how bad it hurt to just watch her, but he didn't know how to 'attack' this problem.

One morning she changed her routine. After her morning swim, instead of heading to the well area with the rest of the women, she started walking the other way. She walked to the other end of the motu. He watched as she waded into the shallow area that separated one motu from the other, and made her way onto the next beach, where she seemed to be walking with a destination in mind.

Then he realized it. There was just one reason she'd be walking that direction. It was where he lived. She was walking to his place.

All of a sudden he became very anxious. What would she think if she found he'd been following her. She'd think he was crazy, or deranged. How would he explain? He had no idea.

But he did know he had to find a way to get to his place before she did. He waited until she was walking along the beach on the south side of the motu, and swam as fast as he could, trying not to make any noise, and then ran down the north shore, passing her with the palm trees between them. He hit the water between his motu and the one they were on, and swam as fast as he could across the 50-foot gap. Then he ran into the growth on the high ground of the motu, looking back to see where she was.

Just as he turned around he saw her come around the corner of the motu and start swimming toward him. He was panic stricken. What would he do? He had no idea how to talk to her, what to say, or what to do.

He ran to his fale made of palm fronds and went inside. All of a sudden he felt it was too small. Too disorganized! Too dirty. She would never want to talk to someone who lived like this.

He started shoving his shorts and shirts under his cot and tried to straighten out the mess that was his home.

"Ron," Milani said from the opening in the trees, "are you here?"

It was customary for a person to call from a distance, to announce their arrival. But this time Ron found his voice sticking in his throat. He didn't know what to say, and if he did, he couldn't get it out. He stood there looking like a deer caught in a car's headlights, blinded by fear and confusion.

Milani stood for a few seconds and then started towards his hut. He had no door on it, and as she approached the door she saw him standing there with his mouth hanging open. She stopped at the door, resting one hand on the door jam, smiling.

Ron stood there like a total fool. His mouth was hanging open and he was frozen. All he could do was stand and stare at her. In the dark of the hut, with her standing in the doorway and the sun shining through her thin pareo, it was as if she was not wearing a thing.

Ron's mouth dried and he just stood like an idiot. Milani smiled at him. Then she took a hesitant step towards him. He tried to move his lips, but he couldn't.

"This place needs a woman," she said, stooping to pick up an abalone shell he used as a plate, putting it on a shelf. "If I am going to live here, I want three more shelves over here." She pointed to the opposite wall. "And we are going to need a bigger bed. This one will never do."

She walked over to him, standing just inches in front of him. She reached out with her hand and gently stroked his face, as if it were a delicate piece of art. "I have seen you. I too felt something when we were on that boat. If you don't say something pretty soon I am going to have to leave."

Ron felt a tear in his eye and didn't know

why. He didn't know what was wrong with him. He reached out and put one hand gently on each side of her face, pulling her gently to him. Their lips met in as soft a kiss as he had ever experienced, yet it was electrifying. He could taste the sweetness of her, and at the same time he could smell her perfumed essence. Neither of them knew how long they stood there, gently holding each other, drinking in the feeling.

"I love you," was all Ron could say. He had never uttered those words to another woman, and she had never heard them from another man.

"Well," she smiled, "at least I know you can speak. That's good. Because I wouldn't want the man I love to go through life not talking to me." And with that she walked to his cot, clearing everything off of it. Then she turned to him.

"I cannot wait any longer," she said, as she unclipped the shell that held her pareo in place. It dropped to the floor and Ron walked to her in a daze. He started kissing her face, and slowly worked his way down to her dark, full breasts, taking one at a time in his hands and caressing them, covering each one with kisses.

It wasn't until the sun was setting that they walked out of the hut and into the blue lagoon. They held hands like school children, and soon they floated in the crystal clear waters, washing each other as an excuse to be close.

Everything was cloudy in Ron's mind as he

thought back to asking Ione for his daughter's hand. Everything just seemed to melt together, and then they were there, living in what was a perfect paradise for both of them.

Until that research ship appeared on the horizon!

Chapter 15

Our sail back to Redondo from Avalon started
out in a pretty somber mood. As we hauled the
anchor I watched Dick and knew he was in a
turmoil.

"Is there some reason you want to think the
worst of your friend Ron?" I asked. "Because
I know if I was just told the same thing about
you, there would be no doubt in my mind as to
where you stood in the world. How well did
you know this guy?"

Dick thought for a second. I could see him
start to brighten almost immediately.

"Hell, I know him as well as I know you,
and you are fuckin' right! There is no way Ron

is one of the bad guys. No way in hell." Dick stopped for a second to gather his thoughts.

"He is in something and he needs our help. Now let's see if we can't find him and give it to him!"

"Okay," I smiled, "but you gotta hoist the mainsail halyard if we are going to get back and find the guy. Now get to work."

Dick started hoisting the mainsail as I walked back to loosen the mainsail sheet. The big white sail tightened at the luff and I cleated the sheet.

"Okay," I shouted, "Eva, hoist the mizzen halyard! Mia, pull in those fenders. You guys look like you're outta Marina Del Rey or something. Let's get this ship underway!"

The sails filled with the mid-day breeze that always filled in out of the northwest, and we started to heel to starboard. I love the feel of a fresh breeze on the beam. The boat seems to move with a silent power that vibrates through every fiber of the vessel.

As soon as we'd cleared traffic I set our course for Palos Verdes, and we let the autopilot take over. It was another beautiful California day, and the four of us were feeling about as lucky as anyone could feel; a great boat, a great day, and great friends to enjoy it all with. The fact that we all knew we would be getting into something we didn't understand when we returned was pushed to the back of my mind. I was living large and loving life!

The sail lasted all the way to Palos Verdes Point. As we approached the R-10 buoy the wind started to die out. That always happened, and we called it the Palos Verdes Triangle. It's an area where the winds move up to go over the hills that project out into the sea.

As the wind started to die I switched on the Perkins diesel and we started rolling in sail. It's a process that I really get into, trying to guess exactly what order to pull the sails in. First we wrapped the fore staysail. That was a no brainer. And when it comes to no brains, I got 'em!

Next would be either the headsail or the mizzen, depending on where the wind was. As it was almost non-existent and coming right off our butts, I opted for the headsail. I grabbed the furling line and Eva started to ease the headsail sheet. She and I had been sailing together long enough to know exactly the right pressure to apply. Too much pressure and I'd get a hernia trying to pull it in. Not enough pressure and the sail would furl looking like a boa constrictor that just ate Bambi (that'd be a large lump in the center!).

By the time the headsail was in we were right in the triangle; no wind at all. I left the mainsail up to keep us from rolling too much, and we all worked on dropping the mizzen. With the four of us on it we had it dropped, gaskets in place and cover on in just a couple minutes.

We always waited until we entered the harbor before dropping the main. It really does a lot to keep a boat from rolling back and forth, even if there is no wind. As we hit the breakwater and spun the wheel bringing the boat directly into the wind, and as soon as we were directly into the wind, Eva released the halyard all at once. The sail dropped in a pile right on the boom. Since we were in the harbor and there was traffic, I had to steer us around little things like other boats and buoys, so the three of them straightened the sail, put on the gaskets and put the cover on.

As I turned down the channel to my slip, we were shipshape. I really like to come into a marina looking like I've just been on a daysail. It makes me feel good.

We stopped her in the slip and Dick jumped off with the bow line. As the stern came over Eva jumped off with the stern line. In a couple minutes we'd tied her up and run the electrical cord so we'd have power. The phone was plugged in and voila! It was Miller Time!

As we entered the Yacht Club Bar upstairs, Eric Stone was playing his guitar over in the corner of the stage. Being a Sunday afternoon there were a few boaters that had been out sailing or fishing, and it was about half full. Because Eva worked there during the week, she wasn't supposed to drink there when off duty. However, we'd worked it out with management awhile back so it wouldn't be a problem. Actually what happened was, we said okay and started drinking across the parking lot, off property at Rubin's. After a couple weeks Rubin's was doing a bang up business, and the Latitudes & Attitudes Yacht Club Bar was empty most of the time. They finally agreed that the help could drink there off duty as long as they didn't wear their uniform. The uniform was long black slacks and a loud aloha shirt.

Eva walked in wearing her shorts and a halter top. Not only was it not her uniform, it stopped two-thirds of the conversations in the bar. The other third musta been gay or something! She looked hot!

Chris was working that afternoon. She and Eva were good friends. Chris was an attractive redhead with blue eyes and a very attractive figure. She walked over and gave Eva a hug.

We all ordered cold beer, which was pretty much a standard after a day's sailing. As we sat there downing the first one Eric ended his set. He put his guitar on a stand and walked over. "How was the sail?" he asked. "Sure is a great day."

Eric really loved sailing. That was one reason he liked playing at the Yacht Club Bar. He had a Catalina 27, and kept it in the marina. He'd sailed with Eva and I over to Catalina a few times, and when he played at the Harbor Reef over in Two Harbors, sailors would sail in from as far as Ventura and San Diego to hear him.

He took the cold Budweiser that Chris had brought him, and chugged about half of it.

"Man," he said between gulps. "It gets dry up there." He put the beer down for a minute, and then added, "Hey, did your buddy find you?"

We all looked at him. Dick was the first to respond. "What buddy? Did he leave a name?" he asked.

"No, he just walked up as I was unloading my gear. I was just stacking stuff on my dolly when this guy walked up and asked if I knew you." He was pointing at Dick. "I told him yeah, and he asked if I'd seen you."

"What did he look like?" I asked.

Eric thought for a minute. "Dark hair, looked kinda oriental, but had blue eyes," he said.

"Ron!" We all said at once.

"When did you see him?" I asked

"Where was he going?" Dick asked

"Do you know where he is now?" Mia asked.

Eric's head swung around a like a saloon door in a bad western. "Hey, slow down! One at a time," he said smiling. "It was about an hour ago. I don't know where he was going, but he said if I saw you," he pointed at Dick, "and you only, I was to tell you where he would be."

We all sat there, intent and listening. "Well?" we said in unison.

"Sorry," Eric said, "but I promised. Only Dick." He turned to Dick. "Let's go over there for a second," he said, indicating an empty table a few feet away.

We sat there on pins and needles. In a

matter of minutes they were back. They were smiling.

"The guy hasn't changed," Dick said. "I gotta go by myself. He's probably a little nervous, and I need to let him know we're all on his side."

He pulled his cell phone out and checked his batteries. "Treb, you got your phone on you?" he asked. "I'll call you." Then he bent over and kissed Mia, and he was out the door.

I picked up my beer and downed what was in it. "Hey Chris, how about another cold one?" I turned to ask her. As I did I looked out the window and saw Dick walking down the walk in front of the boats. I could tell he was anxious to see his friend. We'd been through a lot together, and it felt good knowing he'd found an old army buddy. I was thinking how much he could answer when we found him. There were a lot of unanswered questions we had.

Then I noticed a movement about 200 feet behind Dick. In most cases Dick was pretty careful, it came from his Ranger training I am sure. I'd always noticed how he was watching out of his peripheral vision. Even with my looking for the motion, I had a hard time finding it. Then I saw him. It was the guy that had been outside the restaurant that afternoon in Avalon.

"Oh oh!" I said. "Looks like we have a little fly in the ointment." I pointed just behind the Rubin's sign, across the street from where Dick had just passed. Just as Eva and Mia looked, the guy moved out from behind the sign and ducked behind one of the palm trees.

"I gotta go!" I said, and headed for the door. I knew this guy was busy watching Dick, but I also knew he was ex-CIA and he'd be watching his backside as well as who he was tailing. I pulled out my cell phone and dialed Dick's number. It rang once and he picked it up.

"Dick," I said before he could say anything. "Keep walking and don't look behind you. Don't change pace. The guy we saw at the Galleon in Avalon is tailing you. He's good. I barely saw him even after I knew he was there."

"Thanks man," he said. "I owe ya. I wasn't watching my six. Guess I'm getting a little soft in my old age. I'll take care of it. Thanks."

"Hey, I want some fun too," I told him. "How about we go play under the pier. It's always pretty deserted in the second level."

He thought for a couple of seconds. "Kewl," he said. "I'll take him for a little stroll down the waterfront, and you cut behind the Blue Moon Saloon. I'll take him through the doorway next to Lou E. Luey's, okay?"

"Done. You'd better put your phone away before he gets suspicious. See you in a couple minutes!"

I stuffed my phone in my pocket, then walked behind the Seaside Lagoon so I would be out of his line of sight. I could see Dick working his way through the outside parking lot. Once I was behind the Saloon I ran as far as I could knowing I was out of his sight line. When I emerged at the other end I saw Dick actually working him away. That gave me a chance to get by Lou E. Luey's and get set for our fun and games.

It wasn't but about a minute later Dick walked through the door. It was the only way into the lot, so the man had to be behind him if he was still following him.

Dick was almost out the far side of the parking garage when I heard footsteps coming into the entrance. I tried to stay in the shadows as much as possible. The next second was an eternity. All of a sudden I could picture me jumping a perfect stranger who was just walking to their car. As the footsteps started to round the corner I was standing behind, I stepped out.

All of a sudden I was in the air. Now for a guy who is 6'4" and 280 pounds, being in the air is a very strange place to be. All I knew was, my feet were in the air, my head was down, and someone was flipping me over their shoulder.

I reached out for the only thing I could reach, which happened to be this guys head, and grabbed it trying to get back into a position where I had some control. I landed hard, but held onto the head. As soon as I was down my reflexes took over and I rolled to one side, just avoiding a knife in my mid-section.

I pushed myself to an upright position, and before I could even focus on my opponent, I was in the air again. All I could think was,

I was about to die. All those years studying martial arts and lifting weights, and some guy that looked like ZZ Top's lead singer was about to turn my head into a mushmellon. I was pretty sure that this might be the last fight of my short and sweet life. I just hoped that I had delayed the guy enough for Dick to make his escape and get to Ron.

I hit the ground and was stunned. I couldn't take a breath and I couldn't move. And then I heard laughter. Laughter? Why laughter? Was I dead? I must be, because one of the voices I hear is Dick's. And he's laughing!

Slowly the movement started to come back to me, but I still couldn't take a breath. I worked at turning toward the sounds, and found myself looking up into a very strange sight; a Filipino with blue eyes.

It was Ron. Dick was standing next to him. They were both laughing. I, of course, did not see the humor in any of this.

As my breath started to go in and out like it's supposed to, I tried to ask what was going on, but I still couldn't talk.

"Treb, this is Ron," Dick smiled. "Ron, Treb."

While I tried to come to a position that was a little less embarrassing than laying face down in a parking lot, Ron explained what had happened. It seems he was waiting to meet Dick on the far side of the harbor, and he saw Dick coming toward him. Then he saw Dick answer the phone, and turn. He figured there was something wrong and checked Dick's six. Sure enough, he saw the guy that was following him.

Once again his Ranger training stood him in good stead. He ducked behind cars and got in behind the guy. It was over in a second. The guy was out cold, and Ron started to come get Dick.

And then I walked into the garage. He was still high on adrenaline; his reactions and reflexes took over. If Dick hadn't seen him and called out to him, I would probably be out like the other guy.

I was getting to where I could stand on my own. "Man," I said. "I thought Dick was fast!"

They both smiled.

"Who do you think taught me?" Dick said.

"Yeah, and he was a suckfish student!" Ron laughed.

As we walked across the parking lot Ron showed where he'd encountered the other man. He was no longer there. That worried us all. He could be anywhere. But Ron was sure he was probably at the local Doc in the Box getting a concussion treated, so we walked back to the Yacht Club Bar.

We met the girls at the club and downed a couple cool drinks. Ron was pretty excited and was very apologetic to Mia. Now that she was about over it, she just smiled and told him,

"Anytime!"

Dick and Ron walked off by themselves, and we all knew they needed a little time together to get things straight between them. Eric had stopped playing, so he came over and took Dick's seat, ordering a cold Bud.

"Looks like you found your friend," he said. "Everything okay now?"

"Yeah," I said. "It looks like we'll get to the bottom of this now."

Dick walked back over to the table, and Ron went down the stairway to the parking lot. "He's got something down there he wants to show us," Dick said. "He's getting it out of his rental car, and then he is going to fill us in on all the mystery."

Chapter 16

Ron was feeling pretty good as he approached his car. He felt for the first time in a very long time that he had friends, family even, and he was anxious to fill them in on what was going on in Fanning.

He'd stumbled onto it quite by accident. He was off on one of the small motus that surround the lagoon of the beautiful atoll when he noticed some strange activity aboard the research vessel that was anchored there. It was named the Hammer. They had taken some dogs ashore on one of the outlying motus and then they placed a small object in the middle of the island. They got into their Zodiac inflatable and returned to their boat.

They didn't notice Ron sitting on the adjoining motu. He'd paddled over on his paddleboard, and it was on the beach on the other side. He'd been laying there on the sand just enjoying the day, when their boat pulled up and dropped anchor.

After they were back on board they paid strict attention to the direction of the wind on their instruments. Someone was always watching it sitting atop their antenna mast.

Having lived on the island as long as he had, Ron knew the trades would set in between 10 and 11 am. Sure enough, at about 10:45 the whole crew lined the starboard rail, watching the island intently.

The dogs on the island were all running around barking, obviously enjoying the freedom of being on land after a long boat trip under God only knows what conditions. Then the dogs started to drop. It was like someone had shut down their systems. One minute they were barking and running, and the next they were laying in a heap on the beach.

Ron took care to stay out of sight. He belly-crawled behind some brush on the motu and continued to watch the people on the research vessel. They had a digital video camera set up on a tripod, and it filmed the whole event. Then, after about ten minutes they loaded two men in white contamination suits into the Zodiac and they motored to shore. Once there they walked around the motu, which was about 100 feet in diameter, and seemed to be testing the air with an instrument. After they had walked the complete little island they took off their hoods and waved at the people on the research vessel, giving an obvious all clear.

A little later Ron told Milani about it, and they discussed what could be going on, but neither really knew. Over the next few days he kept an eye on the vessel. He tried to run into any of the people off the boat when ashore, but he realized that they didn't go ashore. None of them. That was very strange.

The boat stayed there for almost a week without having any contact with the natives. Since Ron had lived there so long, they looked at him as one of them, and whenever he'd run into a local they would ask him if he knew what was going on. He didn't.

He decided that he should try and find out what was going on. He told Milani he had to make sure they were not up to anything funny. One day he loaded up his gear and anchored his small boat far enough away from the vessel so as not to be noticed. Then he rolled over the side with a tank on and went down far enough where he thought they wouldn't see him. As he surfaced beneath the boat he swam around to where the anchor was to see if he could overhear anything, and was met by three men holding guns on him.

Ron ducked under the water and swam

straight down a hundred feet, then made for his boat. When he reached his anchor he started up the anchor rode, and suddenly it came loose in his hands. Someone had cut the rope. He looked up the 50 feet to the surface and saw his boat being led away by a Zodiac.

Checking his air gauge he calculated how much down time he had left. If he could control his breathing he figured maybe 20 minutes. His years as a diver paid off as he started to slowly stroke for the nearest atoll. Occasionally he would glance up, and he could see the Zodiac was following his bubbles. He knew he was in trouble.

Then he got an idea. He continued to swim in the same direction he was going and unbuckled his buoyancy compensator. As he moved he adjusted its inflation to give it neutral buoyancy. That way it would stay at the same depth as he released it. He was close enough now to the pass where the current was catching him. He released the BC and air tanks after taking a deep breath, and started swimming in the opposite direction while the current took the air bubbles into the pass.

Ron swam until he thought he could go no further, and then he used an old Navy Seal trick he'd learned while training in the Rangers years ago. He started to go up, and as he did the air expanded in his lungs as the pressure dropped. When he was at about 15 feet he felt a little better, and swam another 25 yards before he had to come up. He was hoping they would be watching his air bubbles and wouldn't see him surface. Sure enough, as he looked back at where they were, they were all intent on the air bubbles. He took a couple of good breaths, and then went under again and made his way behind another motu.

As he sat on the beach getting his breath, Ron tried to figure out just what was going on. Fanning was a pretty primitive island. They only had one ship every six months scheduled to bring supplies in to the 900 people who lived there. As it turned out, the boat ended up coming in about every 18 months instead. There was one Ham radio, and they were pretty much out of touch with the world except for that.

After nightfall Ron swam back to his shack. He filled Milani in on what he'd found out. They knew the researchers couldn't know who Ron was because they didn't know anyone on the island. They never went ashore. That would work in his favor.

The next day he found his boat abandoned by the largest motu, near the one passage that allowed entry to the lagoon. He decided he'd be better off not to get in it, as they were probably watching. Being outsiders, they had no way of knowing the Polynesian culture. No one owned anything. If you wanted to use something, you used it. It was very common for someone to "borrow" his boat, or for him to use one of theirs. He did worry that someone might unknowingly go to use his and end up "missing." But he'd have to think of that later. Right now he had to figure out what these folks were up to.

He walked to the hut where the Ham radio was. Milani's father, Ione, was the only person on the island who knew how to work the radio. He was sitting in the shade on the porch. Ron walked up and sat down beside him. He was used to island time, so he knew he would have to get into whatever he wanted very slowly, or he'd be considered rude. They talked of the fishing, and how Milani was doing.

After a few minutes of idle talk Ron got the feeling Ione was trying to say something, but was hurrying through the pleasantries first. At last he got to the point. It seemed that someone had gone into the radio shack the night before and removed some parts from the radio. Ione might have been the only one who could use the radio, but he did not know how it worked or what was missing. All he knew was it wouldn't work anymore, and he found two screws missing from the back of the radio. Someone had messed with it.

Ron tried to console the man, but his mind was busy with something else. This was no coincidence.

Another bit of news was that one of the outer families, Jahon and his wife Isabella, had been found dead in their hut. Nothing was moved and there was no sign of violence. They were just found by their daughter, who recently married and had moved in with her husband.

As Ron walked back down the beach he saw one of the young villagers running toward him. He was very agitated. The boy was starting to stagger as he approached Ron, and before he got to him he dropped to the ground. Ron ran to where the boy fell, and Ione came running from the radio shack.

As Ron got to the boy he was still breathing, but he was shaking as if he was freezing. His eyes were wide open, and as Ron lifted his head onto his lap he heard him say, "They die." And he did just that. He died.

Ron & Ione sat there looking at each other. They looked down the beach and there were four more bodies laying along the waters edge.

That night Ron tried to assess what was going on. He was sure the research vessel was causing this, but he had to find out how and why. He had to protect his new-found happiness. His wife and her people were not able to protect themselves against armed men.

At midnight Ron made his way around the lagoon until he was nearest the Hammer. Then he slipped into the water. All he carried was a large knife, just in case.

He swam out to the vessel as quietly as he could, and when he was alongside the stern he climbed quietly up on the swimstep. He sat there for a minute while the water dripped off him, and he dried in the warm evening air. He could hear a conversation on the aft deck, but he didn't recognize the language. He was fluent in English, Spanish, Thai, and knew smattering of French. This was none of those.

As Ron listened a man came out of the pilothouse and spoke in English. Ron figured he was one of the crew and didn't speak whatever language it was they were using. It was then he recognized it. They had been speaking Farsi. That was the language of the Middle East.

"Sir," the man said, "I just overheard a radio message from a nearby sailboat. They were trying to raise the radio on the island to see about entering the bay. They say they'll be here about dawn."

A man with a very heavy Mid-Eastern accent answered, "Contact them and tell them it is clear to enter. See if you can get an estimated time they will arrive. This could be very good for us."

"Yes sir," the crewman answered and returned inside.

"Good," the man continued in English. "Now we can test it in the open air!" And then they lapsed back into Farsi.

At dawn Ron watched as a group off the Hammer boarded their Zodiac and headed for the pass. He watched to see if he could figure how many were left aboard. It looked like one in the pilothouse and one deck hand. He figured that there was at least one more full-time crew, but didn't know where he'd be. He might be in the Zodiac, which would simplify things for Ron.

He swam quickly to the boat and climbed onto the swimstep. He heard someone on the aft deck and peeked up over the rail. There was a small man bent over some equipment fiddling with something. Ron quietly jumped the rail and hit the man with a sharp jab right above the carotid artery. He dropped like a sack of potatoes.

Ron stealthily made his way up the ladder to the pilothouse and saw the captain of the boat concentrating on a new weather fax that had just come in. Ron opened the door and before the captain could turn around he'd brought him down as well.

He looked out to where the Zodiac had gone and saw that they'd moved ashore just inside the pass. He noticed them fiddling with some equipment. They were all wearing white hazardous material suits. Just then he saw the bow of a beautiful sailboat coming around the entrance to the lagoon. It had one man up on the lower spreaders watching for coral, and a woman on the bow pulpit. As they started their way into the pass they waved at the men in the white suits on the beach. They must have thought it odd to see men dressed like that in a tropical environment.

Before they had a chance to consider what they were seeing, the man atop the spreaders started to crumple to his knees and then fell off the mast. At about the same moment the woman on the bow folded double over on the rail. The boat started a slow turn to port and hit the waiting reef, lodging between two outcroppings.

The men on the beach quickly loaded their equipment aboard the Zodiac and started back to the Hammer. Ron wasted no time. He ran from cabin to cabin searching for some kind of clue to these guys' identity. In one cabin he found a metal case with five small vials of a white powder marked TEST. The case had places for eight. There was also a map of the United States open with weather charts and notations. This was not looking good.

Ron knew he had little time to waste. Falling back on his CIA training, he did his best to memorize the charts and maps he was looking at. Then he pocketed the metal case and started out of the room. Just as he was about to turn out into the companionway he heard footsteps. There must have been a third crewmember after all.

Ron had to find out who these guys were. He heard the man about to pass the doorway, so he jumped out and jammed his hand deep into the man's solar plexus. He gasped for air and went to his knees. Ron stepped behind the man and whipped his knife out, holding it under the man's throat, letting the blade cut into his skin.

"Okay, who the hell are you and what are you doing killing innocent people?" he asked, not really expecting an answer.

The man was still gasping for air, and Ron knew he didn't have much time left before the other men returned to the boat. He moved the knife up to the man's right ear and deftly cut it off. The man screamed and grabbed for the side of his head.

"Now, God damn it!" Ron shouted. "Where are you from?"

The man was whimpering, "We're from Hawaii. This is a research project. Honest. Just a research project." He wiped his bloody hands on his pants and looked up at Ron.

"Who are your passengers? Where are they from?" and Ron put his knife under the man's other ear. "Now. Who are they?"

The man pulled back in horror, thinking of the loss of his other ear. "Okay, okay! This is a research project for the US Government. I swear. Don't cut off my other ear. The boat was chartered to a government agency. All I know is we were to be here for another week, and then head back to Hawaii."

Ron threw the man to the floor and headed down into the engine room. He picked up a large crescent wrench as he entered the room and started smashing whatever looked like it would break. Then he grabbed a razor knife from the toolbox and started slicing hoses. The third time was a charm. Salt water started flowing into the boat. He finished cutting the five-inch line to the water for the exhaust and went back topside.

Lined up against the port hull were 10 five-gallon gas cans. It was obviously fuel for the dinghy. He jabbed his knife into the bottom of two of the cans, and gas started to flow onto the deck.

There was an electric winch cable running across the deck to a hand-held switch which was hanging by the rail. It was used to raise and lower the Zodiac dinghy. He quickly grabbed the cable and cut deep into the insulation, pulling two cables out and dropped them into the flowing fuel. Then he placed the switch box over the side near the back of the boat.

The Zodiac was almost there. He had to take a chance. He worked his way to the opposite side of the boat from where the Zodiac was approaching and dove in. He dove underwater and swam under the boat and came up right behind the Zodiac as it tied up. He held his breath and waited for what seemed like an eternity, but in reality was probably more like 45 seconds. The movement on the Zodiac had stopped. It was now or never.

He swam up under the Zodiac and took out his knife. He jabbed it into each of the buoyancy tubes on each side and the one in the front. He reached up and grabbed the hoist switch and flipped the power on. He heard the whoosh of a ball of flame and the horror in the screams of the men who had just boarded. Then he took a deep breath of air and swam for shore as fast as he could.

Chapter 17

· ·

Pizzaro sat in his room at the Portofino and was taking some aspirin for his head. It hurt. Whoever had jumped him knew what they were doing. He was hit from behind in the parking lot with so much force he blacked out. When he'd come to there was no sign of the man he was following. To top it off, when he'd checked in with his superiors he was told he only had a couple more days to complete his task or other methods would be found. That would mean he'd failed, and Jim Pizzaro did not fail.

He sat watching *Lost Soul* knowing that

eventually they would have to return to it. As he sat he tried to think of what he might have missed. He'd gotten the sample of Zyron back when the stupid people at the civilian labs sent it to a government lab. Since 9/11 all government labs had to report any suspicious materials to Homeland Security, which meant the CIA, NSA and other law enforcement agencies. As soon as the NSA got the report they had him go into the lab and confiscate it for "National Security."

In the years Jim had worked for the NSA he came to realize just how convoluted the US Government really was, and just how naïve he'd been for most of his life. One of the first jobs he'd been given was to help with a bombing of the US Embassy in Israel. It seems the powers that be felt Israel's plight would be able to gain a lot more support if the US was attacked on their soil. In order to justify large shipments of arms, they needed a little arm twist in Congress. What better way than to have a couple of US soldiers go down in the fight?

Having been with the CIA for so many years he'd been toughened against some of the things that the good guys did, but once he switched to the NSA he learned just how these guys' minds worked. They would pretty much take both sides of a fight so either side that won, they'd be on it. Just like in Central America in the '70s and '80s.

Of the two groups, Jim decided the NSA was the sneakiest, and that's where he found his home. He liked thinking like they did. It just made a good fit. It didn't bother him that he was following, and planning to kill, a man who he'd worked with in the CIA years earlier. He had a job, and this was it. That was why he'd been chosen for this job. It had been years ago, but still, he would know Ron Tess when he saw him. That gave him an edge. In a business like this, an edge was a very good thing.

The further you got into the covert end of the NSA, the fewer the people who would know about a particular objective. These days, with such big money being paid for "inside story" type books from retired government agents, they had to be a little more careful than they were in the days of the Contras and Sandinistas.

The splinter group he'd been assigned to had a pretty simple job. They were to test this new poison that they had just completed. It was called Zyron and it was a powder that was innocent until it was introduced to a little oxygen. Then it would expand into a nerve gas, and it was instantly fatal to any living organism.

They found one of the most out-of-the-way islands on earth, Fanning Island, and were undergoing tests when, of all people, Ron Tess turns up living there. No one knew where he'd gone after he'd left the CIA, and quite frankly, no one cared. He had too many scruples for undercover work anyway.

The tests on the island were going as

planned. The powder was so concentrated that just a pinch, when exposed to oxygen, would turn to gas. When breathed in it would seize the whole nervous system instantly. But soon after Zyron was infused with oxygen, it would turn back to a harmless powder and drop to the ground. It would dissipate so that, even in an autopsy, nothing would be found.

The dogs they'd taken were used first, but they found they were using too much of the Zyron powder. It had taken almost five minutes for the excess to dissipate. They tried it again on one of the smaller motus and it worked perfect. Death was instantaneous and you could walk the area in just 30 seconds after it was released.

Everything was going well with the tests when Tess had shown up. The final test was when the boat, Julia II, had entered the lagoon. They'd set up 200 yards down wind, and it worked instantly. Now they were ready to move on to a small American suburb outside Atlanta, Georgia. When the cry about terrorism on U.S. soil settled, the President would have the ultimate power he wanted. Then he could do pretty much whatever he had in mind to take over the uranium deposits in Swahala.

Pizzaro saw nothing wrong with this plan. He knew that the ends always justified the means. The sheep that were always bleating about human rights and such things had never seen what he'd seen. They just didn't know what was right for them. He would help to set things right. But first he had to stop Ron Tess from blowing the whistle. Jim knew that without the sample of Zyron, his story would be just that. A story. No one listened to malcontents, and if they were ex-government employee whistle-blowers they were listened to even less.

He was looking out the window of his room, keeping an eye on the *Lost Soul*, when he saw a man walk out of the bar and toward the parking lot. Looking closer he saw that it was none other than Ron Tess. Sore as he was, he got out of the chair and made his way to the door. He ran down the stairway and made his way out into the lot. This was his chance and he had to take it.

At the bottom of the stairway he went out the back door and worked his way around to the side of the building to where he could see the parking lot. Tess had just closed the door to a car and was walking back to the bar entrance. Pizzaro worked his way between the cars, keeping low so as not to be seen.

As Tess walked up to the stairs, Pizzaro was just about to use his lead-filled blackjack when Robert, the concierge, walked out of the bar door. "How are you doing Mr. James?" he asked.

Ron looked back and saw Pizzaro about three feet behind him. The leather covered blackjack was in his hand and there was no doubt of his intentions. Ron dropped to his left in a roll and came up off the ground with a spin-kick to the man's face. In a matter of seconds the man laid on the parking lot, out cold.

Robert stood there in shock. The folks in the bar heard the commotion and were jammed in the doorway all trying to get out at once.

When they made it to the bottom of the stairs, Robert had come out of his shock and was starting to move toward the lobby to get some help. Treb stopped him.

"Robert, hold on a minute," Treb said, "You know this guy?"

"Yeah," Robert stammered, "that's Mr. James. He's in 327. Been here a week. He's a good tipper."

Treb walked over to Robert's side and put a hand on his shoulder. "Robert," he said, "this is not a nice person. Just forget what you saw here. Trust me. You'll be better for it," and he reached into his pocket and handed the man a $20 bill.

"Uh, sure Treb. No problem," and he walked off, a little bewildered.

Dick and Ron had picked the man up and were heading toward the elevator through the rear entrance. "Come on," Ron said, "let's see what we can find out."

On the ride up in the elevator they searched him and found his room key and a 9mm automatic. Dick took the gun and Treb opened the door to the room with the electronic key. He was starting to come to as he hit the bed, so Dick cut the light cord and tied his hands to the bedpost, cutting the cord from the blinds to bind his feet. By the time he was fully awake he was helpless lying on the bed.

He glared at Ron. Ron looked back with a look of dawning recognition. "Jim," he said slowly. "Jim Pizzaro. You're the one who's been trying to kill me? What the hell is this all about?"

Treb and Dick just stood there wondering pretty much he same thing. "You know this guy?" they asked in unison.

"Know him? Hell. I used to work with him," Ron said. He explained how he'd been working with the CIA in Cambodia and Thailand after he escaped from the prison camp in Viet Nam. The CIA wanted him because he spoke the language so well and could fit in. He continued the story until he got to the part where he left.

"I couldn't put up with the fact that we were financing both sides of a losing battle," Ron said. "The poor people were the only ones losing. The upper echelon would take money, the US would give arms to both sides, and the poor people would die fighting for nothing. So I left. From what I heard, this guy," he nodded toward the man in the bed, "he left the CIA too. I thought maybe he got smart too. But it's starting to look like he went to the other side."

Pizzaro glared at Ron. "Fuck you," he spat. "You were such a pussy you just couldn't see what was going on. Sure we armed both sides. That's the only way to be sure you win. You bleeding heart liberals make my ass hurt!"

Treb walked over and sat on the side of the bed. "Buddy, your ass ain't the only thing going to be hurting here. Now who do you work for and why are you trying to kill our friend here?" He indicated Ron. The man turned his head away and said nothing.

Ron started going through every drawer in the desk. Soon Dick and Treb were taking apart his luggage and the rest of the room. They didn't find anything useful.

Ron knew they couldn't call the police. If they did, the police would take him in and a few hours later he'd be out. It was obvious by his attitude that he was still with some government agency. They just needed to find out if it was their government or someone else's.

Treb knew there was just one way to do that. He picked up the house phone and dialed Bob Fox. After a short conversation he looked at Dick saying, "He'll be here in an hour. He's flying over. How about calling Mia and asking her to pick him up at the Long Beach airport?"

For the next hour they listened as Ron explained what had happened on Fanning Island. They were pretty much in shock when they heard about the people being killed so cold-heartedly. Ron told them about Milani still being on the island. He'd had to leave to let people know about what was going on there, but now he knew he had to get back to Fanning.

Chapter 18

. . . .

With the flames still visible on the burning wreck of the Hammer, Ron swam for the channel where the yacht had just gone up on the reef. Some of the islanders had seen the wreck, and they were rowing over in their boats. Ione was one of the first to arrive.

They reverently moved the bodies to the beach while Ron surveyed the damage to the boat. Ron knew he was the only hope of getting off the island and getting the news out about what had happened there. If they'd kill people that easily, then the people of Fanning didn't stand much of a chance.

The reef had put a small crack in the hull

of the boat just above the waterline, where it had laid over against the sharp edges. There was water flowing in and he jammed a cushion against it, lodging it there with an oar from the dinghy lodged against the opposite bulkhead. The batteries were still above water, but it was rising fast and the engine was still running.

Ron shut off the exhaust water intake and disconnected the intake line from the thru hull fitting. Then he dropped the end of the hose into the bilge, and the water pump of the engine started to assist the bilge pump in getting the water out of the boat.

As the water lowered in the boat and the weight was lightened, he could feel the boat start to move against the reef. He got to the deck and unlocked the windlass, releasing the anchor. He got Ione to pull one of the small boats under the bow, and take the anchor out to the middle of the pass where he threw it over, and then dove in to make sure it was set.

As soon as Ione surfaced and gave the thumbs up, Ron engaged the windlass taking up the slack on the chain. Inch by inch he would tap on the windlass switch, and inch by inch the boat pulled off the reef. In a few minutes it was free. Ron pulled the anchor up and motored inside the pass, anchoring in the shallows near the first motu.

He and Ione were joined by Victor. Victor was the Matai, or head of the village. The research ship had sunk in about 50 feet of water, and there were two survivors. One was badly burned and wouldn't make it. The other would be okay in a few days.

Ron figured he'd better get out of there as fast as he could, and take the samples with him to see if he could get them to the CIA for testing. He was sure this was some terrorist organization, maybe even Al Queda, from their speech. He had to warn the U.S. He didn't want to leave Milani, but he knew he was the only one who could get the word out, if anyone could.

He looked the boat over. It was a few years old, but looked like it was well kept and in great shape. It was a Moody 64, a good bluewater boat with all the latest equipment on it. The hole was superficial, and he easily repaired it with a two-part epoxy he found in the tool locker. The Ham radio and SSB were the best money could buy. That was the good news. The bad news was, the hole had been right above them, so they were both useless as tits on a boar hog.

The boat was provisioned for three people who would not need the provisions anymore. Everything else seemed to be in fairly good order.

Ron made a snap decision. His years in the Rangers and CIA had made that a way of life. He turned to Victor and Ione. "I am going to take this boat to Hawaii and see what I can find out about the research vessel and the people on it. Try to keep the survivors here as long as you can so I can get a good start. If there are no boats coming in for a while, I might be able to get there before they can radio for help. Then he looked at Ione. "It might be a good idea to "lose" a few of the parts to the radio, in case they try and fix it." Ione agreed with a smile and a nod.

After agreeing on the plan, they separated and went to get some coconuts and bananas aboard, and fresh water from the rain catch. Ron knew he'd be at sea for a time. His biggest hope was that no other boats would visit the island for awhile, giving him more time to get to civilization.

Ron swam ashore and ran back to his shack. Milani was waiting on shore as he swam up to their motu. "I saw the fire, I was so worried" she said, running into his arms.

He explained what had happened, and then he had to tell her the hardest part. He told her about Jahon and Isabella being found dead. Milani and Isabella were the same age and had been raised together. They were best friends and she broke down when she heard the news. Their world was falling apart and her heart was breaking. She didn't know about war and killing. She didn't know how mean people could really be. He had wanted to keep it from her, but he couldn't now. The world had invaded his personal paradise, and he knew he had to do something to try and save these beautiful people.

Ron held Milani as she sobbed, and as the sobbing subsided he took her gently in his arms, kissing her wet cheeks. "I love you. You know that, right?" He looked deep into her eyes. She just stared at him with a questioning look.

"I have to go," he said, hating to have to say it. "I have to go and find out who these men are, and make sure there are no more like them coming. No one else can do it. I don't want to leave you, but I have to do what I can to stop this from happening to others."

He stood and watched her face. At first she started to cry again, and then a look came across her face that reminded him of the day she came to him and said they would live together.

"You will go and stop others from being hurt." A glint was in her eye. "Then you will come back here so we can finish our lives."

She kissed him gently on the lips, and almost crushed him with her arms. She then released him and turned, walking back to the hut. She stopped in the doorway. "I will build the shelves tomorrow I think." She smiled at him and then continued. "You will return when you can. My love knows this."

As Ron walked into the water to swim back to the boat, he was thankful the saltwater of the sea washed away the saltwater of his tears.

In less than an hour Ron was out of the pass and sailing north. He held that course until the island was out of sight behind him. Then he tacked and started on an easterly tack. He knew the Equatorial countercurrent ran right along here, and he knew he could get a two- to three-knot push eastward.

He felt bad about lying to his friends on the island, but in case the survivors were able to fix the radio, he had to make them think he was sailing north to Hawaii. Instead, he planned to ride the countercurrent as long as possible, and make directly for the U.S. mainland and California.

The people who owned the boat, which was named Julia II, were very capable sailors. That was obvious by how well the boat was equipped. He felt a pang of regret when he was looking through their documents and came upon their passports. Greg Jacobs and his wife Ann were accompanied by their son Luke, who was just 19 years old. According to the ship's log they had set sail from San Diego almost a year earlier and were planning to head to Hawaii to sit out the hurricane season and then sail back to finish a circumnavigation of the Pacific.

The winds were starting to freshen and Ron adjusted the sails accordingly. He had sailed some in his youth and remembered the drill. Also, the years as a fisherman gave him an insight into the seas and the weather patterns. He spent the first few hours trying to figure out all the instruments, and after awhile he settled into a routine.

On the fifth evening out he was motoring along in a dead calm. He'd left his sails up to catch any wind, but he had entered the doldrums. The autopilot was handling the steering, so he dozed in the cockpit, waking every once in awhile to check the horizon. He was way off the shipping lanes, by plan, and didn't expect to see much of anything, but he'd always believed in 'better safe than sorry.'

About ten minutes after he'd checked the horizon, he'd just fallen back to sleep when his world turned upside down. All of a sudden the boat was lying on its side and he was thrown against the lifelines and almost went overboard. The winds were blowing at 45 knots and his sails were all up. He tried to get up, but the boat was still laying on its side with water running down the companionway. He knew he had to do something, but he had no idea what. He was trapped against the lifelines with water pulling at him, trying to pull him through the opening. Thinking about how Milani was waiting for him, he held tight.

As fast as it hit him, it stopped. The boat sat upright and the winds were calm. He looked around him and could see nothing in the darkness, just some whitecaps off behind him. As fast as it had come up on him, it had gone.

He didn't sleep anymore that evening. At dawn he looked around and saw that he was surrounded by tall white columns of clouds. Under each column was a sheet of rain falling, but there were great gaps of sunlight between them. This was the heart of the doldrums. Feast or famine. Too much wind or no wind. He was crossing the Intra-Tropical Convergence Zone. The ITCZ. He'd heard of it, but this was his first experience with it.

He checked his position on the GPS and found the pilot chart for that month. Sure enough, where he was crossing the equator the ITCZ was about 200 miles across according to the charts. That meant he had better motor due north to get through it. Then he'd be able to sail, even if he'd have to tack against the wind.

He knew he'd have to start conserving his fuel. He'd read the manuals and knew he had about 125 gallons with a full tank, and he found the ship's log showing they'd filled up in Pago Pago. They had a good sail up to Fanning, so he still had about 100 gallons of fuel.

According to the engine manual it would be the most efficient at 1400 RPM. He would burn about 1.2 gallons an hour at those RPMs. He checked his speed at 1400 RPMs and found he averaged about 6.6 knots. That meant he had about 80 hours, or about 500 miles of motoring.

The generator burned about .75 gallons an hour, and he knew he had to run it every once in awhile to keep the batteries charged when he was sailing. He decided he would run the generator at least one hour every day.

Having estimated the voyage to take four

or five weeks, he knew he was going to have to conserve. That meant he had to get out of the doldrums so he could sail. Luck was on his side, and less than two days later he hit the wind. He figured he had about 45-50 gallons of fuel left. It was going to be close.

The next 10 days he sailed tight into the wind. He found the boat would hold a pretty good speed at about 33° off the wind. Day after day he pounded into the seas, and every night he would reef the sails down, just in case. He'd learned his lesson about squalls.

He was about 500 miles from Catalina Island when he ran out of fuel. He'd been running the generator and had the watermaker turned on, filling his water tanks. He only ran it every other time, because the extra current-draw burned more fuel. One minute it was humming away happily, and then it died. He went below and pulled the inspection plate off the fuel tank. Sure enough, it was dry.

He checked the water tanks and found he had a little over half of one tank. That meant about 50 gallons. More than enough for one person for a long time. He had found two five-gallon diesel jugs in the lazarette, and he planned on using them when he had to maneuver into a port.

For the next couple days he had enough wind to sail, and then the high moved in over him. The seas calmed and the winds died. The flap, flap, flap of the mainsail as the boat rocked back and forth was maddening. All he could think about was those poor people whose dream had been to sail the world, and how their lives had been cut short "as a test." He vowed to do something about it.

It took him almost a week to do the last 500 miles. After the second day his batteries started to die and he turned everything off. Once a day he would flip on the power just long enough to read the GPS. He sat becalmed for a couple days, and then a slight breeze started. As soon as he felt the sails start to fill with wind he was on deck. He put up every inch of sail he could find. The slight breeze, maybe three knots, moved him along at a snails pace, but it moved him. The first day of the breeze he only made about 50 miles. Then it started to fill. Pretty soon he had five knots of wind and he was starting to move.

With no batteries his autopilot was out of order, so he practiced tying down the wheel at different angles to see how long he could get the boat to go in one direction. He never could get it to stay long enough for a nap, so he stayed awake as long as he had wind.

As he came in past Point Conception it was as if the country was welcoming him home. A full breeze, 15-20 knots, filled his sails. He felt as if he was flying. As he passed the west End of Catalina he broke out the fuel cans and poured them into the tank. He went below and bled the lines. The generator had its own battery, and it came to life. He watched as the batteries started to fill, and soon the engine came to life.

He pulled around the west end of Catalina and found a place to anchor off Indian Rock in Emerald Bay. It was just 30 feet deep with a white sand bottom and he went below and fell to the bed, exhausted. He slept for a whole day. Then he made the call to his old friend Dick, Bondano.

King Harbor

Chapter 19

Bob Fox walked into the Room 327 of the Portofino Hotel and found Treb, Dick, and their friend Ron, sitting on the balcony overlooking the marina. On the bed was a very upset Jim Pizzaro. Bob Smiled at him as he passed, and walked out to the balcony, pulling up a chair.

"Ron," he said, holding out his hand, "it's a pleasure to meet you. My name's Bob Fox."

Ron stood up and took the big man's hand. "Dick's told me a lot about you," he said. "I guess we have the same alma mater?"

"Yeah," Bob answered. "I think I just graduated a little before you. I'd like to ask you a couple questions if you don't mind." He looked at Treb and Dick. "You guys mind giving us a minute?" Treb and Dick walked back into the room, closing the glass door.

"Okay, what the fuck you guys think you're going to do with me?" Pizzaro asked. "I do work with the good guys ya know!"

They ignored him and walked to the TV, turning it on. They found CNN and pulled up a couple of chairs from the dining table. "Good thing they got him a suite! Nice comfortable place to hang out, don't you think?" Treb said.

"Yeah," Dick answered, "and such a nice view of the marina, and your boat."

Just then they heard a muffled conversation coming from what they thought was the next room. "Hey. That sounds like Eva and Mia," Dick said. "They in the room next door?"

They got up and walked to the closet door. When they opened it they found the radio receiver and could hear Eva and Mia talking clearly. "Hope the boys are alright up there," Eva said. Then Mia answered her. "Yeah, when Dick's in a hotel room he turns into an animal," she laughed. They'd just got back from picking up Bob Fox at the airport and were on *Lost Soul*.

Treb looked at Dick as Dick picked up the house phone, dialing the boat. All of a sudden they could hear the phone ringing in the radio. "Hello," said Eva, answering the phone.

"Tell Mia I didn't turn into an animal," he laughed into the phone. "I'm just an old hound dog, looking for a place to bury my bone!"

"How did... What...?" Eva stuttered.

Dick cut her off. "This asshole had the boat bugged. We don't know what else, but we're checking now. See you in a bit."

Bob and Ron were walking in from the patio. They looked rather incongruous. Ron was slight and wiry, maybe 5'6" on a good day, and Bob Fox was like an old bear, 6'6" if he was an inch and as large as a grizzly. At that moment Treb and Dick couldn't tell you which one they'd rather have mad at 'em, but one thing was sure, you wouldn't want them both mad at the same time.

Bob looked at Treb and Dick, smiling a most wicked smile. "Hey guys, you mind excusing me and my partner here? We have a little extraction work to do here, and neither of us thinks you should be witness to such brutality. We know how sensitive you are."

Treb and Dick smiled. Treb answered first. "Couldn't we just hold the branding irons or something? This could be fun!"

Dick chimed in with, "Yeah, I could peel some bamboo strips, maybe go get the car battery and jumper cables?"

Jim Pizzaro's eyes were as wide as 1961 Plymouth hubcaps.

"No thanks guys," Ron answered. "We are trained professionals," he smiled. "But don't try this at home!"

Treb and Dick walked to the door, opening

it. "Okay, we'll be down on the boat looking for microphones and other such shit. Give us a call if you need any help hauling body parts out." And with that, they smiled and walked out the door.

Once back at the boat, Dick called his studio. One of his assistants had a sideline de-bugging corporate offices. Not extermination, more like getting rid of electronic bugs. In a few minutes he was on his way to the boat.

Treb and Dick sat down at the salon table going through all the crap they'd found in the closet with the bugging device. There were two briefcases stuffed with crap. They laid it all out and were going over it piece by piece when the girls put a plate of sandwiches in the middle of the pile.

"Okay, you guys need your strength so you can beat up bad guys and have mad passionate sex with your girlfriends. Eat," they said.

About thirty minutes later Richard Cortez showed up at the boat. He was the de-bugging expert. He opened up his satchel and pulled out a couple of little devices and started walking from cabin to cabin. He found two audio bugs in the main salon, one in the upper steering station, and one in the aft cabin. When he told them that was all there was, Treb and Eva looked at each other.

"You mean he could hear us in the aft cabin?" Eva asked, eyes wide.

"Honey," Treb answered, "people all over

the marina could hear us in the aft cabin the way you carry on!" They all laughed. Eva just sat there and blushed.

The boat's phone rang and Treb picked it up. He listened for a few seconds and then put the receiver in the cradle. "Bob and Ron are on their way down. Looks like we're going for a little sail," Treb said. "Richard," he continued, "what do we owe you for checking the boat out?"

Richard held up his hand smiling. "Hey forget it. If I didn't do it Dick would cut my hours at the gym. I gotta get back to class." Then he turned and looked at Dick. "But I am still on the clock, you know." And he smiled as he hustled up the gangway and off the boat.

"Okay guys, let's prep the boat. It looks like we are going out for a little day sail," Treb said, and he headed topside to start removing sail covers and undoing the dock lines.

They pulled out of the slip just as it was starting to get dark. Bob had instructed them to pull into the fuel dock. The dock was closed for the evening, and there weren't a lot of people around.

As soon as they were secure to the dock, Ron started down the walkway to the dock pushing one of the laundry carts from the hotel. He was wearing a hotel uniform and name tag. It said his name was Martin. Bob Fox was a little ways behind him, carrying a small briefcase. When they got to the boat Treb and

Dick jumped down onto the dock.

"We gotta go out a little ways and dump this body," Bob said, winking at Treb and Ron. "Do you have an extra anchor?"

Treb saw the laundry bag move and heard a muffled sound from inside. He caught on. "Yeah," he said nonchalantly, I've got an extra 90-pound Danforth and a 66-pound Bruce. Which one do you need?"

Bob thought for a minute and then said, "Probably both. We'll need one for each piece. You do have a sharp filet knife don't you? And maybe a hack saw too?" The bundled moved a little more violently.

After they had their "bundle" aboard, they cast off the fuel dock and started out the channel. They sailed out about 10 miles toward Catalina Island and then dropped the sails. They were all alone in the middle of the Catalina Channel.

"This should be good," Treb told them. "The current runs pretty strong through here and the next time he touches land it should be about two miles from here, straight down."

"But wait," chimed in Dick. "I thought there were great whites out here. You think we need to waste the anchors?"

They all stood around deep in thought, while Pizzaro, who had been un-bundled but was still tied and gagged, lay on the deck between them. He knew that Fox and Tess were both ex-CIA, as was he, and they now knew that he was with the NSA. He was sure they were just trying to scare him. They wouldn't hurt him... would they?

"Yeah," Treb said. I forgot about the great whites. Those anchors cost money. Let's try this first." With that he walked to the cockpit and loosened his mainsail sheet. "Hey Dick," he hollered, "Unhook the mainsail sheet from the traveler. We'll tie a rope around him and do a little shark trolling!"

They could all see his plan, and they moved Pizzaro under where the end of the boom would be over the deck. Then Ron tied a line around the man's ankles and hooked the shackle at the bottom of the sheet to the line. Treb started hauling in on the sheet and the man hoisted off the deck like a flaying Marlin.

Bob Fox got serious for a minute. "Okay," he said, "we need to find out what those fuckheads in Washington are up to. After what I saw in Central America in the '70s, and what Ron saw in Indo-China in the '90s, there is no telling just what the fuck these NSA guys are up to."

"How do you want to handle this?" Treb asked.

"Like this," Bob said, and he started to swing the boom out over the ocean. He cut the gag off of Pizzaro's mouth saying, "We gotta make sure he can talk." And then he started to lower the man into the water head first.

They were drifting slowly, with just the evening breeze pushing them. Ron reached into his pocket and pulled out a knife. He reached out and deftly sliced the hanging man's chest just deep enough to make him start bleeding. The blood started to drip into the water and all of a sudden Pizzaro was not so sure they weren't really going to kill him and feed him to the sharks.

Dick and Treb held the end of the sheet line, alternately dropping the man upside down, waist deep, and then pulling him out. They all knew the blood in the water and his thrashing would draw sharks.

Dick was the first to see the thrasher shark as it made a pass just under the hanging man. He reached for his Pelican dive light and lit it up as it swam back and forth below Pizzaro.

"That's a pretty good size shark," Treb said. "What do ya think? Six feet? Seven?"

Bob Fox seemed to be considering the question. "Looks like about seven. But they eat real slow." He was looking into Pizzaro's eyes. "I'm glad it's not a great white. They eat way too fast. They don't seem to enjoy their meals like the thrasher."

He waited a few seconds, and then addressed the man hanging out over the water. "Okay," Bob said in a soft voice, "for the sixty four thousand dollar question, what were you guys doing killing those people on Fanning Island, and who were the Arabs that were with you?"

Treb started to lower him back into the

water just as the shark was making a lunge. All
of a sudden Pizzaro screamed. "Alright! Get
me outta here! I'll tell you, I'll tell you! Just
get me outta here! But you're not going to like
it!"

King Harbor

Chapter 20

Jim Pizzaro was still bound and laying on a bunk below decks. He was not a happy man. As he tried to think back he started to realize his predicament. The whole team he'd assembled for the project had been pretty well knocked out when that damned Ron Tess stumbled on them doing their test in Fanning. Who would have thought that out there in the middle of nowhere there would be an overzealous patriot running around?

The plan had been formed over a period of about a year. It was basically a sound one, or so he thought. They wanted him to create and train a small team of four or five Middle

Eastern types to perform an act of terrorism on U.S. soil. They could then blame it on the small, newly formed country of Swahala. That was all he'd been told. It seemed easy enough. He was told of this new chemical formula that would kill quick and easy. All he had to do was find a few people willing to sell their souls for American dollars, and then do the deed.

He had found two brothers from what was now Swahala. They were in Folsom prison. They had been caught smuggling heroin into the country. When caught they had fired on the DEA as they were breaking in and killed one of the officers. That gave them the death penalty. When he'd offered them a secret pardon and deportation to the country of their choice, they'd jumped at the offer. That was the start of his little team.

It was a simple plan, and it would have worked if only that damned Tess hadn't been on the island. They were on the last phase of testing. After their research vessel had burned and sunk, there were only two people left alive, himself and the younger brother, Ahmed Vassili. They had managed to get ashore, but both were badly injured. Jim came out of a deep coma after about two days. The brother who'd survived with him passed away the night they washed ashore.

Jim found out that Tess had floated the boat they'd put on the reef, and he'd sailed off. He knew that his life depended on finding him.

Being a totally covert operation, he couldn't just call for help. No one knew of this operation except for the director of the NSA. He had to find a way to stop the man from blowing the whole operation. In other words, he had to get off the island and find him.

It was a week before any other boats visited Fanning Island. It was a Japanese fishing boat. They planned on fishing the waters for about three days and then heading to Tarawa in the Gilbert Islands to offload their catch. Pizzaro contacted the captain and arranged for passage.

Once in Tarawa he got to a radio and made contact with the NSA. An Air Force C-130 was diverted on a trip from Guam to pick him up, and in a few days he was back in Washington, DC sitting in the NSA Director's office waiting for the Director, who was in a meeting somewhere else in the capital.

Bob Clark, the Director of the NSA, left the President's office and felt as if he'd just been scolded by his mother. It was humiliating. Here he was, head of one of the most powerful agencies in the world, and he was berated because one stupid underling had fucked up. He had to make this thing work.

The President wanted to attack Swahala. It was a small and unimportant new country that had formed itself south of Ethiopia. No one paid much attention to the place. A lot of heroin was coming out of the country, but nothing like the amounts that were coming out of Asia, so it was unimportant. But then Uranium was discovered out there in what had to be the most useless area of the world. General Umboda, the dictator of the new country, was trying to play the U.S. against China in getting the funds and equipment to mine the rare ore. The bidding was getting to be a little more than he felt like paying.

The President had a better idea. The U.S. was the most powerful country in the world, and if they planned to keep things that way they would need to keep that uranium off the world market. It was in the interest of national security, he assured himself. There was a clear and present danger if that uranium was to get into other's hands, right? At least that was how he'd justified this operation.

The plan they had worked up seemed to be a good and logical option. They would covertly set up a small group of people from Swahala to perform a terrorist act. They'd just have to kill a few people on U.S. soil and the American people would "force him" to retaliate. He called in Bob Clark, the head of the NSA and an old friend and ally. They discussed the situation over a long lunch, and a plan of action was worked out.

And so Jim Pizzaro was given his assignment. Why they wanted to attack a small town in the U.S. wasn't Jim's problem. He was just ordered to make it look like Swahala did the attacking. That should have been easy. The Zyron from Dr. Boredanski had just been formulated and no one knew of its existence other than the NSA people who had financed the project. Once it was complete, all records of the manufacture of this deadly material had been destroyed. It could never come to light that this was developed in the U.S.A. It would have to look like it was developed outside, by terrorists.

It was up to Clark to find a way to put the blame for whatever happened elsewhere. He was good at that. It was his job. As Director of the NSA his whole life was hiding things and making people believe whatever it was the President wanted them to believe. This was just another exercise in deception and misdirection.

"What kind of a clusterfuck have you gotten us into?" Director Clark asked Pizzaro. He didn't really expect an answer, but he knew they had a real problem going.

"Look," Jim answered him, "how the hell was I supposed to know there would be some fucking whacko Rambo loose on the island? Our research showed the place was perfect for our tests. We did exactly what you wanted. The chemical worked perfect, and the release mechanism we designed was as good as you could want."

"Yeah, right," Clark said. "And all you had to do was get your team back here to drop a few friendlies, and we would have been home free. But no, you had to play Terry and the Pirates on a desert island in the middle of bumfuck."

Pizzaro knew that the man was pissed, and he also knew the man's reputation for getting rid of incompetents. He had to redeem himself in his boss's eyes. He had given it a lot of thought in the week it had taken him to get back there. He had his plan, and he just had to get a little assistance to make it happen.

"Mr. Clark," he started, "I have a plan that I know will work, and we can still complete the mission. I just need to find where the man brings the boat in. I don't know who he is, but once I find the boat I can find him and we can blame the whole thing on him."

He then explained his plan. After he took care of this "small problem" he would take a salvage boat back to Fanning and bring up the rest of the chemical and the release mechanisms. He'd finish the test on that remote island, and then complete his mission.

Bob Clark sat there thinking. This man had screwed things up pretty bad, but at this time it looked like he was their only way to finish this.

"Okay," Clark said. "I'll give the Coast Guard a call and have them find the boat. But then you are on your own. Get the job done, and get it done fast."

At first the Coast Guard searched the waters between Fanning and Hawaii. That would have been his most logical direction. Searching millions of miles of water is no easy task, and it took them a week just to give it a cursory inspection. They had no luck.

The search went on, but the job of finding a lone sailboat in the Pacific was a pretty daunting task. The search continued for weeks to no avail. Then one morning the Coast Guard found the boat as it was entering U.S. waters off Catalina Island in California. They were told not to hinder the vessel, and Jim Pizzaro was on a plane to LAX within the hour. His plan was simple. He'd kill whoever it was that had screwed with his team, get back the samples he'd stolen, and then recruit another man from Swahala. The country was poor and there were drug runners getting caught all the time. He knew it would be easy.

But first he had to find whoever it was that had done this and see what he knew. Then he had to finish the test. That would be easy. As soon as he got rid of this pest he would be ready. At least that was what he'd thought at the time.

And now he was bundled up like a prize pig on the way to market. He had been so scared when he'd seen the shark he had blurted out about the test in Fanning. He told them the truth, but not all of it. He said he'd been hired by the Swahala terrorists to train them and help them get into the U.S. after the test...

...and they believed him.

King Harbor

Chapter 21

. . . .

On their way back to King Harbor Treb told Bob Fox he'd better call his friend in Washington and let him know what was going on. He was sure when the U.S. heard about this terrorist threat it would be handled. For the first time in weeks he was actually starting to relax.

Bob Fox called Val Strasser on his cell phone. It was one in the morning in Washington, but this had to be told.

When Strasser answered he was still deep in sleep. It took him a couple seconds to come around. Then Fox told him what they'd found out. He told him all about the Swahala terrorist plot to kill Americans. Strasser listened to the whole story, and by the time Fox was through speaking he was as awake as he could get.

"Are you sure of this?" he asked. "This is some pretty heavy shit. You say you have this chemical there with you?"

"Yeah," Fox said, "we have five vials of it, but there is more on the boat that sank in Fanning Island. You need to get to the director and get his ass out of bed. We need to get a plane out there and secure this shit before someone else does."

"Okay, I'm on it." Said Strasser. "It shouldn't take more than a few minutes, and I'll get back to you. Be sure to keep this guy Pizzaro on ice. We'll need him."

As the *Lost Soul* made her way toward the harbor, everyone on board was silent thinking about what they had found out; a terrorist plot with a new chemical that was virtually untraceable. They knew the U.S. would want to get their hands on it and get it out of circulation.

The lights of the city were like a pile of jewels in the clear night as they motored toward it. They reflected on the windless waters, and everyone was deep in thought. The silence was broken by Fox's phone ringing.

"Yeah, Fox here," he answered.

He listened for almost a full minute, then he simply answered, "Yeah. Right. I understand," and hung up.

Bob sat for a few seconds, seeming to get

older before their eyes.

"What was that all about?" Treb asked.

"Yeah, what's up?" asked Dick.

Bob looked very tired. "They told Strasser to drop it," was all he said.

"What do you mean, drop it?" Treb asked.

Ron Tess stood up and walked over to Bob, putting his hand on the old man's shoulder. "You mean it's ours?" he asked him.

Bob looked up at him and there were tears in his eyes. "Yeah," he said. "It's us. The test was a U.S. action. They were testing a new chemical warfare agent. We sent them. We killed those people in Fanning. It was another one of those NSA/CIA miscommunications. The man at the top, the President himself, called the CIA director and Strasser into his office in the middle of the night and told them to just forget it."

Treb and Dick just sat there. It hadn't sunk in yet. This was too much to accept so fast.

"You mean our government was killing people as a simple test?" Dick asked, incredulous.

Ron answered him. "Yeah. Just like the shit that was going on in Thailand and Viet Nam after the war. That was why I left the company. It just didn't make any sense."

"Same thing happened in Central America back in the '80s," Fox added. "That was why I finally left. I always thought we were the good guys. Obviously I was wrong." He sat there totally dejected. He looked every bit the 80-year-old man.

It was quiet for about two or three minutes as the truth sank further into their heads. It seemed like an eternity. The sound of the throbbing diesel, the feel of the swaying boat; it all seemed to be a bad dream. Each man had his own thoughts.

"You know what?" Treb asked quietly. "That just plain sucks."

"Yeah," echoed Dick.

"You know," Ron said, "maybe we should just go and fuck up their plans."

Bob Fox looked up at these three men. They might not have youth, but they had experience, and there was an old saying, "Sometimes the cunning of an old man can be better than the strength of a young one."

"You know," he said, "if someone could get to Fanning and get those chemicals before they finish their tests, they might be able to stop this shit."

"It's not like we are dead," chimed in Ron.

"All we'd need is a good plan," said Treb.

All of a sudden the atmosphere on the boat was charged with electricity. They started to bounce ideas off each other, and soon a plan was formulating that would have made any chess player proud. The years of service to their country were going to pay off. Their training helped them know just what "the other guys" would do. They knew, without a doubt, the reactions that the government would have. They knew because until just a few minutes ago, they were "them." Now, all of a sudden, they were a team and the operation was forming.

"You know they will be watching our every move to make sure we are going to drop this thing. How are we going to get to Fanning? If we fly, they will track us. We need to get them on a false track. I've got an idea," Fox said.

As he was the most experienced of the group, they all listened. After all, for years he had formed operations that were successful. "They wouldn't be trying to track you if they thought they knew what you were doing, right?" he smiled.

"Yeah, but how..." Ron started, and then he stopped. He snapped his fingers and pointed toward the foredeck. "You mean...?"

"Whatever we want to tell them, we can just tell them... through our tied up friend below," Bob said.

Treb said, "He'd never believe anything we said. Besides, I had plans to drop him as we pass the wreck of the Dominator. There are always some good sized sharks hanging around there."

"What if we let him overhear our 'plans'

and then he 'escapes,'" both Bob and Ron said in unison. Both had a lot of experience in misdirection. After all, they had been trained by the best.

"He'd have to believe what he heard, and he'd have to escape on his own. How the hell could we arrange that?" Dick asked.

By the time they were passing the point that Treb had wanted to drop him overboard, the plan had been arranged. Treb and Dick went below with Bob Fox. They sat at the navigation station in the salon. Their bundle was wrapped in the forward cabin with the door closed, but they knew he could hear them. Bob started.

"So, I guess we should let the asshole go," said Fox, loud enough to be overheard.

"Let him go?" Treb asked. "Are you fucking nuts? That butthead tried to kill us all. Let's just dump his ass overboard. It's too far for him to swim. They'll find his scrawny ass floating in a few days."

"Look," said Dick, "I know we can't do anything about what he did, but can't we just dump his ass overboard? It's bad enough knowing we must let this shit go. I want at least a little blood for the trouble he's caused." He hesitated, "How about we take a vote?"

They all went up the companionway smiling. After a suitable time Dick and Treb went below and grabbed Pizzaro. They drug him up the companionway and threw him onto the deck. As they manhandled him, Dick was able to ease the line they had tied his hands with, and it went unnoticed.

"Take off his blindfold," said Ron. "I want to watch his eyes when he dies."

Bob undid the blindfold.

"Okay asshole," Treb said, "you wanna live the life of a terrorist? How about seeing if you die well? This might make it a little easier for us to take. We hope you had a nice life, because it's over now!" With that, he pushed the man over the rail.

There was a better than average chance he would make it. If they had made it too easy for him to escape, he'd suspect something. This way, they hoped, if he lived, he would tell his superiors they had accepted the official version and would leave it alone.

Chapter 22

A lot of people aren't aware that the waters off of Southern California are pretty chilly. The Alaskan current rushes south through the San Juan Islands, and then down the coast of Oregon. As it passes San Francisco Bay it's about 48 degrees. By the time it hits Point Conception it may be up to 50 degrees. Once it's made it by the Channel Islands it is about 52-55 degrees. That's pretty cold for swimming.

When Pizzaro hit the water he thought he was a dead man. He had pretty much accepted that when they had taken him out on the boat. He'd not expected to return alive.

As the cold Pacific water hit him he felt

a shock. It was probably about 55 degrees, and that was very cold when you just fall in. He struggled to make his way to the top and then he thought better of it. If he popped right back up they might shoot him. If they thought he'd drowned they might sail off. He held his breath and tried to look around in the dark waters. His chest was still bleeding and he was afraid sharks would be attracted. About 20 feet away was a large bundle of kelp. He wiggled and tried to make his way toward the semi-safety of the seaweed. As he reached the edge he slowly surfaced. He tried to hold his head as flat as possible so he could breath through his nose, and so they wouldn't see him. He could still hear the thump of the motor, but it was moving away. The buoyancy of the seaweed helped keep him afloat.

The bindings on his hands were starting to work loose. As they did he started to work at them. He had no way of knowing it was because Dick had started to untie the ropes as they dropped him overboard. The buoyancy of the seaweed helped him stay near the surface as he worked at his bindings. When free he untied the gag, and then the line around his ankles. He looked toward the lights and estimated it was about a mile. He knew he could swim it if he wasn't hit by a shark first.

He started to slowly stroke for the shore. He started with a kind of a sideways dog paddle so he wouldn't open up the gash on his chest.

He vowed as soon as he finished his assignment he would kill all of these people.

The swim took him almost 40 minutes. By the time he was climbing out of the water the *Lost Soul* was docked. Bob was already at work on the phone. He called Strasser to let him know that he was heading back to Catalina. The CIA had to think they had dropped the whole thing. He knew they would be trying to watch them for a while, so he got to work laying the smoke screen they had planned.

Meanwhile, the boys started to ready *Lost Soul* for an extended ocean voyage. They serviced the engine and brought on all the spares that were kept in a storage space. As they did that, they had the girls start supplying for a long cruise.

Treb contacted some old friends from his previous life when he was a biker and rode with the Warriors. He called on his old friend Matt. They had been through a lot together in the old days, and he knew he could count on him.

After a few hours there were three of his old riding partners sitting in the Warriors' clubhouse. All three had spent time in Viet Nam in the old days, and he knew he could count on them. He told them all about the testing, and then about what was happening on Fanning Island. While they talked they had a couple of cold ones. It was almost like old times sitting there in the clubhouse, and Treb liked the feeling.

"Ya know," said Matt, "Big Paul was asking a lot of questions about you and Dick."

Treb remembered Big Paul as a guy who used to ride with them on occasion and was always having problems. "What kind of questions?" he wanted to know.

They filled him in a little, and by the time it was over Treb was pretty sure Big Paul was a pipeline to Pizzaro, somehow.

"Tell you what," Treb said to them, "get hold of Big Paul and tell him you heard that me and Dick were going for a little ride up to Sturgis. Tell him we were planning on going over Berthoud Pass, over the Rockies."

They finished their planning and Treb got on his bike and headed back to Redondo. As he felt the life come into his bike, he sat back into the comfortable seat and turned out onto Beach. He wicked the throttle a little and felt the throb he loved to feel. His fishtail pipes echoed off the store windows as he passed, and once again, he was feeling alive.

He turned onto the 91 Freeway and kicked through the gears. When he was up to 65 he held her steady. He didn't want to be stopped by some overzealous cop. He had a lot of work to get done.

As he made the transition from the 91 to the Harbor Freeway, he did manage to find a short space where he knew he was pretty safe and he turned the throttle on full, feeling himself pushed back into the seat with the wind in his face. He was living and loving life.

The transition from the Harbor to the San Diego Freeways brought him back down to reality. He was soon getting off at the Crenshaw off ramp and heading down 190th street. As he came over the last hill before the beach he looked out over the ocean he loved so much. He knew that his friends were waiting for him on the boat, and he made a quick trip along PCH instead of riding down Harbor Drive, where all the bikini clad skaters slowed traffic to a crawl.

On the boat the supplies were being put in their places. She was sitting a little lower in the water than she was earlier.

.....

After Jim Pizzaro had made his way ashore, he sat on a bench on the strand, soaking wet. He had to formulate a plan and he had to do it fast. Things were starting to get too much out of his control. As the sun started to rise and light the water, he went into the public restroom. He took off his clothes and passed them under the electric hand dryer until they were dry enough to wear without drawing attention.

He walked along the strand to the Redondo Pier, and then made his way to the Portofino. He found Robert at the concierge station. It was hard to believe it had only been a day since he'd last talked to him. It seemed like it was ages, and he felt a lot older.

When Robert saw Pizzaro he hailed him. "Mr. James, that cab driver, Big Paul, called trying to find you a few minutes ago." He stopped. "Mr. James, what happened to you? You look terrible. Anything I can do?"

"Yeah," he said, "I lost my key. Can you let me into my room?"

"No problem, sir. Follow me!" and he led the way to the elevator.

Once in the room, Pizzaro picked up the phone and started making calls. The first was to Bob Clark in Washington.

"What the fuck have you been doing out there?" was the first thing he heard on the phone when Mr. Clark picked it up. "The President has been all over my ass like stink on shit. Now what the fuck happened?"

Jim tried to put it as easy as he could, but he soon found out that the CIA had to be brought in, and this thing was getting way out of hand.

"We have had to move up the 'event'," Clark told Pizzaro. You have one month, and the deed has got to be done."

Jim made some mental calculations and felt that might not be enough time, but knew better than to tell his boss that. "Okay Boss, you got it," was all he said. Then he told Clark what he'd overheard on the boat. "I don't think they are going to be any trouble, but we had better watch them to make sure. Can you give me a couple people for that? Maybe three? That should do it." He didn't tell the man what he had in mind for them after it was all over.

That was private business!

"Okay, I'll get a couple locals. I'll e-mail you their contacts. Let 'em know what you want." Clark hesitated and then continued, "But you get your ass on a plane and get the fucking job done. My ass is starting to hurt from having bites taken out of it!"

A few minutes latter, as Pizzaro was eating his breakfast sent up by room service, the phone rang. It was Big Paul. "You said if I learned anything about Treb and Bondano it'd be worth something," the man said. "What's it worth?"

Pizzaro didn't feel like playing games. "Look dickhead," he said, "If you know something tell me, and I'll make it worth your fucking while!"

"Well," the man started, "I heard from a couple of their old riding partners. They said that Treb and Dick were all pissed off about something, and that they were planning to take a ride up to Sturgis, South Dakota, to get it outta their systems. Seems they used to go there every year, and they just wanted to get away."

"Any idea when they planned on leaving, or what route?" Pizzaro asked.

"Yeah," Paul continued, "they were leaving fast. Like this afternoon. They were planning to ride through Colorado, up over Berthoud Pass. That's all I heard."

"Okay," Pizzaro said, "I'll leave $100 with Robert for you in an envelope. Let me know if you hear any more."

"$100?!" Paul shouted into the phone. "A lousy $100? That won't even pay my bookie! I thought you were big time! I ain't putting my ass on the line for no $100! I want a grand!"

"Fuck you," said Pizzaro. "There'll be $100 here for you. If you don't want it, fuck off!" and he hung up. He was tired of people shouting at him.

So they were going for a little ride, huh? He picked up the phone and called the first of his new agents. He told him that there were three bikers heading out for Berthoud Pass in Colorado. He told them when they were leaving, and told them to, "take care of them." They could figure the approximate time, and he gave the man a description of Treb, Dick and Ron, as well as a description of Treb's and Dick's bikes. With that he called his other contact and told him to follow Bob Fox over on Catalina until he could get back. He needed to make sure he had truly dropped things. He made a few more calls and soon he was packing. He had to get to Hawaii to find a salvage vessel.

Chapter 23

. . . .

A pair of eyes was watching Ron as he walked across the Portofino parking lot. Treb and Dick were waiting by their bikes. They had borrowed a third bike from Matt's shop. He had about three or four that were for sale, and they picked one that looked like it would be comfortable for a long putt. They had packed the sissy bars with their stuff, and their sleeping bags were tied to the handlebars. It was obvious they were off on a long trip.

Dick stood up to kick his bike to life. He was the only die-hard who insisted on the old kick-starter. Not only was it a kick start, but it was a left hand kick start with a suicide clutch.

The other bikes were electric start. As soon as Dick's bike roared to life, Treb and Ron hit their starters and the roar of Harley's filled the lot.

As the bikes rolled out of the lot and headed toward Catalina Avenue, a lone man sitting in the room rented by Mr. James picked up a cell phone. "Okay," the man said, "they are on their way. You should be able to pick them up at 190th & Hawthorne. Three of them."

A new set of eyes picked them up as they crossed Hawthorne Blvd. and fell in behind them in a nondescript Ford. He followed as the bikes entered the freeway.

Treb looked over at Dick and smiled. "Man!" he hollered to be heard over the roar of the pipes, "why don't we just keep on going. Fuck this being heroes."

Dick smiled. "Sure, like you'd pass up a chance to kick some ass! Right! Maybe after it snows in hell, but not today!"

Ron pulled up between them in the lane. "We got a shadow!" he hollered. "Just like we figured! Tan colored Ford Taurus, about six cars back!"

Treb was amazed that he could have spotted the tail with a vibrating mirror, but it had been his way of life. He nodded, and his mind returned to the problem at hand.

When they hit Beach Blvd. they pulled off the freeway and rode up to the Warriors clubhouse. They were careful not to lose their tail. Once they were in the parking lot of the closed clubhouse Ron watched to make sure they were seen. He made a slight nod when he saw their tail, and they walked over and unlocked the clubhouse, walking in. As soon as they were inside Treb walked over to a window that had been painted over with black paint, and peered out through a scratch in the paint. He could see the tan Ford parked across the street.

A few minutes later they walked out and mounted their bikes. Once again Dick kicked his bike into life, and Treb & Ron started theirs once the first bike had come alive. Then they turned the bikes back towards the freeway and started the long ride to Sturgis.

The man in the Ford made note of the time they left and followed. If he'd stuck around about 15 minutes he would have seen the same three men, in different clothes, walk out of the clubhouse and get into a F-250 Crew Cab pickup. It belonged to Matt.

"Well, it looks like they went for it. It'll be a few hundred miles before they realize they are following your clothes and bikes. It's a good thing we had three members that were built like you guys," he smiled, poking at Treb. "We almost had to dress two people in your clothes."

They drove in silence back to Redondo Beach. They would wait until after dark to return to King Harbor, and the waiting *Lost Soul*.

Bob Fox knew how the CIA and NSA

worked. They wouldn't waste a lot of manpower watching "possibles." Their concentration would be on completing the task. He was counting on them still using the same parameters now as they did when he was with them.

Bob knew that he was being watched just as they all were. Since Treb, Dick and Ron had lost their tails, it was now up to him to get his as busy as possible. He left *Lost Soul* just before sunset. He walked slowly to the lobby of the hotel and asked them to get him a cab. Robert was on duty, and he whistled for a cab waiting around the corner. When it pulled up Bob got in. He said, loud enough to be heard by the concierge, "Catalina Express off the Harbor Freeway in San Pedro." He knew a blind man could follow him, and he wanted to make it easy for them. As the cab pulled out of the parking lot, the last pair of government eyes left the Portofino, and King Harbor.

A little after dark a boat very similar to *Lost Soul* turned into the King Harbor Marina. While Treb, Dick & Ron untied the *Lost Soul*, the look-alike motored in their direction with Sluggo at the helm.

When they saw the boat coming around and into the channel, Treb put her into reverse and backed her out of the slip. He took her down the side channel and waited while Sluggo pulled the other boat into its place. Treb didn't know how Fox had managed to find a similar boat on such short notice, and he didn't really care. This was the only chance they had to make this work.

Sluggo tied the boat down with the lines that *Lost Soul* had left on the docks, and he ran to the edge of the dock and dove in. With strong strokes he swam to the aft of the real *Lost Soul*, and Dick dropped the ladder to help him aboard.

Now they were complete. All they had to do was sail across three thousand miles of ocean unseen, and then take out a whole team of NSA agents. How hard could that be?

Chapter 24

Ron Tess was on watch. They had been out for three days and he figured they were well out of U.S. waters by now. They had not seen any other vessels. Their first tack was out past the west end of Catalina and on past San Clemente Island. The shipping lanes went down the California coast, and then slipped between the Channel Island chain and the mainland. That kept them out of the big seas. In order to keep from being seen, the *Lost Soul* had to go where others wouldn't. That meant they would purposely go where the seas were known to be rough.

Since they had to sail south to get well

into the easterly trades, the seas didn't affect them too much. Even though they were running at a steady 8-10 feet, the wind kept them rolling along and the seas were very manageable.

It was his favorite time of the night on the boat. He had rotated into the midnight until 2:00 am slot. All his sailing days, this and the 2:00 am until 4:00 am slots were what he liked best. All the others aboard would be asleep, and it was just he and the sea and the stars.

He looked at the instruments and all was well. They had about a 25-knot evening wind behind them, coming from about 140 degrees, and the seas were running with them. He could feel the surge as the swells would pass beneath the boat, picking it up and kinda 'tossing" it forward. He watched the knotmeter as it would surge up to 10 and 11 knots down the face of a wave, and then slow to 8 and 9 when they slid down the backside as it passed under them.

The stars were crisp and clear. He looked up and saw Orion and greeted him like an old friend. This was where he was always the happiest, at sea, far from the games that people play. Far from what people laughingly called civilization.

He had learned years ago that the most civilized people on earth were those who were called uncivilized. That thought led him to think of Ione, back on Fanning. He would be considered uncivilized in any city. After all, he couldn't read. He couldn't write. He'd

Bob Bitchin

never seen a television, and he'd never read a newspaper. He wouldn't know the business end of a gun if it were pointed at him. Uncivilized. Yeah, he thought, but one of the most civilized men I ever knew. In the years he lived on the island Ione and he had become friends.

That was pretty much why he'd settled on a place like Fanning Island to make his home. The people. He loved those people and their simple and honorable ways.

He listened to the sound of the ocean's waves passing beneath him, and for the first time in a long time he was feeling at rest. He noticed a slight motion in the dark of the cabin below, and Treb came up the companionway.

"So what do you think? Did Popeye have it right, or what?" the big man said, smiling. Ron could see why his old friend Dick had become so close to this man. He was easy to like.

"Yeah, a man could get used to this," Ron Replied. "Too bad we have to be in such a hurry. I could take a little of this life."

"Well," Treb said, "from what we can piece together it looks like they must have had at least another five or six pounds of the powder that Pizzaro called Zyron on board that boat. If what he said was true, that's enough to off half the population of the southeastern U.S. We know he survived his little evening swim because we were being watched the next day. So there is very little doubt but that he will be

195

heading back to get what was left in the hold of the Hammer and continue his mission."

When they had finally gotten Pizzaro to start talking, he didn't stop until he realized that they weren't going to feed him to the shark. By then it was too late. They had learned about the whole plot. Everything except that it was being setup by the NSA, and they found that out later with the help of Bob Fox.

They knew they couldn't fly in to Hawaii or Pago Pago and charter a boat. The Government would be watching the airports. Their only chance was to sail there. It was at least a three-week voyage, but once they were gone and another boat was in *Lost Soul*'s slip they figured their odds were not all that bad.

They couldn't take a chance and radio Bob Fox. There was no doubt the airwaves would be monitored. They just had to chance that they'd have enough time to get there. And meanwhile they were enjoying a great sail. The wind had freshened to 30 knots, and it was coming right over their shoulder.

Ron was about to get off watch, and he asked Treb if he wanted help to reef the sails before he went down to turn in. "No, we need all the speed we can get," the big man said, "and besides, were just starting to get some good speed."

By the time Dick was coming on watch the wind had continued to freshen, and was up to 35 knots. They were making a steady 12-

13 knots, and Treb decided they had better reef the main before they started to broach when they were surfing down a wave's face. It was still dark, but they worked as a team. Treb turned the boat up into the wind long enough for Dick to ease the main halyard. When the first cringle of the reef was down far enough he hooked it onto the reefing hook and cranked the halyard tight. Then he wrapped the first reefing line around the boom halyard and cranked her tight. It only took, at the most, two minutes. The years they had sailed together off the coast of Southern California were paying off, along with the many deliveries Treb had made when Dick could get away and play crew. They loved sailing and the sea.

Treb turned the boat downwind again and she fell into the groove. Before long they were once again doing 12 knots, but the boat was handling a lot easier. It always amazed Treb that reducing the sail could, in some cases, actually increase their speed.

The blow continued as they sailed south and west, heading doggedly toward their destination, the tiny island known as Fanning, just a little south of the equator.

Chapter 25
. . . .

The salvage vessel Maverick was motoring through the pass into Fanning Island with Captain Mike at the wheel. On the bow a very anxious and nervous Jim Pizzaro was trying to will them faster into the lagoon. It had taken almost a week to get the boat and have it provisioned for a voyage to Fanning. No matter how much he tried to hurry the skipper, he just did what had to be done. Captain Mike could not be prodded, and his was the only salvage ship available on such short notice.

The voyage down had taken almost five days. The steady thumping of the huge diesel never ceased. It just kept thumping, and the boat moved along at its own speed, eight to nine knots. That was what she did, and no one seemed to notice that as being out of the ordinary except Pizzaro. He only had a total of three weeks to get the final test accomplished and his new team to Valdosta, Georgia, for the "terrorist attack."

It didn't take a rocket scientist to figure he wouldn't be able to make it. He had called his boss, Bob Clark, on the phone three times on the crossing, but the man wouldn't budge. He needed the "incident" to happen on schedule. It was imperative. What Clark hadn't told Pizzaro was there would be a meeting of the full Senate two days later, and the President had planned to announce the invasion of Swahala at that meeting. The timing was all-important.

As the boat entered the lagoon he tried to remember exactly where the other boat had gone down. He looked at the chart and tried to figure it out, but it had been dark and he wasn't sure. He knew the general area and pointed the skipper in that direction.

The boat moved across the clear blue waters of the lagoon and soon they were dropping their hook. It was deep, almost 120 feet, but the 150-pound Bruce anchor dropped to the lagoon's floor and dug in.

It was just before sunset when they shut the motors down. Captain Mike went through the shutdown procedures like an automaton, flipping switches, turning on the generators and killing the big diesels. He turned on the engine room vents and started down the companionway to his cabin.

"Where are you going?" asked Pizzaro. "We need to find that boat!"

"I'm going to my cabin," Captain Mike said. "I'm going to get a good night's sleep. The boat will be easier to find in daylight. Specially at this depth."

"I thought you had sonar on this tub?" retorted Pizzaro. "You don't need light for that. We need to find that boat, and we need to find it now!"

The Captain looked at the annoying man with a look of distain. "Look, I am going to sleep. You should too. Tomorrow is going to be a big day." And with that he turned and left the room.

Pizzaro stood there and fumed. Then he turned and walked to his cabin. He paced for almost an hour, and then gave up and turned in.

.....

At just about the same time the S/V *Lost Soul* was doing close to 10 knots on a broad reach just 80 miles off the island. No one was more amazed than Treb, who happened to be on watch at the time.

"This is one hell of a sail we have going here," he said to Sluggo, who was sitting in a bean bag chair hunched over a bowl of chili, which was their bill of fare for the evening meal.

"No shit, Sherlock," Sluggo replied. "We have had more 200 mile days this trip than I have since I started sailing."

A 200-mile day was a milestone that sailors on small vessels could count on one hand. It was just an average of a little over eight knots, but it was a constant eight knots. For a voyage of this length most skippers would be happy with one or two 200-mile days.

Treb knew they had been pushing it, but they had stitched six consecutive 200-mile days together and then topped it off with yesterday, a 240-mile day, an average of 10 knots. It was an incredible voyage, and they were all excited about it. They'd almost forgotten their mission and got completely into the sail. They broke out the cruising spinnaker a little after dawn, and soon they were capping the waves and surfing down them at 11 and sometimes 12 knots. It was exhilarating.

But now that they were starting to get closer to their destination they were all wondering just what it was they could really do. They had no idea of how many people were there, or if they were too late. Maybe the government had flown in two weeks ago and gotten the rest of the Zyron.

The sun was just setting and Treb was coming off watch. Everyone else had eaten, and now, as Dick took the wheel, Treb went below to get a bowl of hot chili. Ron was at the stove heating up another pan-full for him. They'd run out of onions a week earlier, so it was just chili with some grated cheese on top; a simple meal, but one that would hold them through the night.

"Okay, here's your little farter starters," Ron said, handing him a steamy bowl. "If you put enough cheese on it you might be able to make some bricks in the morning."

Treb took the bowl and sat down at the salon table. The boat was rolling as they made way, so he put his foot up against the bulkhead to keep himself in place. It was a move that was second nature to him; he'd been at sea for so long.

"So, Ron, tell me," Treb said between bites, "what are we looking at tomorrow. We should get in around dawn. Is there any way we can get in and not be seen?"

Ron had given this a lot of thought, and had already formulated a plan. "Here's what I was thinking." He grabbed paper towel off the rack and a sharpie from the navigation station, and sat down at the salon table. He drew a quick sketch of the island. The ink from the Sharpie soaked into the paper towel, but you could make out what he was drawing. It was a rough sketch of the island. Then he put an arrow. "This is where we should approach from. There is a large stand of palm trees and we should be well hidden from any sighting from the lagoon."

He hesitated for a second, seeming to be thinking about it, and then continued. "Of course, if it were me I'd have lookouts on duty all over the island, so the chances are we will be seen. If that happens we could be in big trouble."

Treb pulled a chart of the island out from the chart holder below the table. He unrolled it and studied it for a few minutes. Sluggo came down the stairs from above decks and walked over looking at the chart. "That the island?" he asked.

"Yeah. That's it," Treb said. "What do you think?"

"Well," he said, rubbing his chin, "I'm not a big time spook like these guys, but from a collector of squishies and squigglies, I think I'd anchor off here a ways," he indicated a shallow reef about two miles off the island, "and then I'd take the dinghy in. Be harder to spot than a big old boat with a big stick sticking out of it."

Ron and Treb looked at each other, then at the chart, and then at Sluggo as he walked to the stove and started scrapping the leftover chili into his bowl. "The other anchorage just doesn't look right," he said to no one in particular.

Chapter 26

Milani had been watching for every boat that approached Fanning Island, and each one had to be the one Ron was on. After a couple months she still came out for each new boat, but less with anticipation and more with the resignation that he had probably decided to stay in "his world" instead of coming back to this barren desert island.

Her father, Ione, felt he would return. He kept her spirits up by telling her this, and also telling her how much Ron had agonized over making the decision to leave. Every morning, when she would awake in their hut, she would look to the doorway and see him standing there, looking at her, as he used to do every day.

On the day the new research vessel entered the lagoon she had a feeling of dread. This boat was larger than the first one, but the people on it acted the same way. They didn't come ashore, and they avoided the people of the island. This wasn't a normal way for people to act. After a long spell at sea, usually people went out of their way to come ashore and seek out others, even if just to find out what had been happening on the island.

She tried to imitate Ron and do as he did when he had been keeping an eye on the other boat. She did the same. She watched them as they maneuvered over the area the other boat had gone down. They motored back and forth for the first day they were there, and then they got all excited and started hollering at each other. She knew they must have found the sunken boat. Of course she had no idea why they would want to find it. That didn't matter. In her mind she knew Ron would want to know what was going on if he were to return, and so she set her mind on trying to find out as much as she could.

The following morning she went to her father and asked to use his fishing pram to do a little fishing. Ione had thought this very strange, as Milani was never into fishing, but he thought it might be good for her to take her mind off her missing husband.

As she pulled away from the beach and

hoisted the single small sail, he looked down
and saw that she hadn't taken any of his fishing
gear with her. But she was already out of
earshot. He would make it a point to talk to her
when she came back, to find out just what she
was really doing.

He walked out of his hut, and all of a sudden
he knew she was about to get into trouble. During
the night another salvage boat had entered the
lagoon. Knowing what kind of people were on
the first one, he imagined these might be of the
same ilk. He searched the lagoon for his pram,
and soon located the white and blue sail he'd
made out of an old potato bag. She was heading
right toward the salvage vessel.

He knew she would be getting into trouble
if she approached the boat, but he didn't want
to holler out, as it might cause her even more
trouble. He had another small pram he used for
fishing off the outer reef, but it was on the other
side of the atoll. He decided he had better see if
he could get it and bring it into the lagoon to try
and stop Milani from getting into any trouble.

The last time he'd fished the outer reef
was about a week ago. He remembered leaving
it tied up to a large piece of driftwood not too
far from their hut, but on the outer edge of the
atoll. As he ran through the forest of palm trees
he hoped that no one on the island had used it
and moved it to where he couldn't find it. In
the old Polynesian custom, no one really owned
anything on Fanning. If you needed a boat, you

used it, and then put it back when you were through. He knew that someone would have used the small boat in the last week, and he just hoped they put it back where he'd tied it up.

As he followed the path across the atoll he started to come out of the underbrush, and he saw the top of the short mast. It was there! He ran to it and quickly untied the rope that held it. Then he pushed it out into the small surf. The outer reef protected the beach from large swells, and he was thankful the surf wasn't too large for him to launch the boat.

Just as he was jumping into the pram he saw something out of the corner of his eye. He turned and looked and couldn't believe what he saw. There was a sailboat anchored outside the reef. He sat back and stared at the vessel. Watching the boat he could see three or four men on the deck, and one of them looked very much like it could be Ron.

He quickly turned the pram and started rowing toward the sailboat. It seemed odd to him that they would anchor out there, outside the lagoon. The anchoring was always much better inside. He rowed, and as he got closer he could see that it was, indeed, Ron. And Ron recognized Ione as well. He stood waving on the bow. As Ione pulled close to the boat he could see that there were three men with him. When he was close enough to talk he started telling Ron about the trouble Milani was getting into.

Ron helped Ione onto the boat and they embraced like family. "Ione," Ron started, "I want you too meet my friends."

The first man he saw was Treb. Ione took a step back and looked up into his eyes. The man was a giant, but his look was one of a gentle man. Ione had never seen anyone built like he was. His arms were huge, and he had tattoos all over his body. In the Polynesian culture that meant he was a man of standing, and Ione was instantly respectful. Treb smiled at him as he shook his hand, and Ione felt a kinship with this large man.

He was then introduced to Dick. Once again he was taken back by the power he could sense in this man who was obviously of Polynesian decent, but who was wound so tight he moved like a cat as he came across the deck to shake Ione's hand.

After he was introduced to Sluggo, they sat in the cockpit rapidly discussing what had happened over the past few months. It didn't take long, and they were anxious to see what they could do to stop the salvage boat from getting the Zyron. And while they were at it, they had to make sure nothing happened to Milani.

They were glad to hear no one had seen them come in during the early morning hours. The fact that there were no guards on the Atoll helped too. They sat and made their plans. Soon Ron and Dick were getting into Ione's pram, and they started sailing toward the entrance to the lagoon.

Meanwhile Treb and Sluggo unloaded the Zodiak and brought the motor up from inside the lazarette. They inflated the dinghy while on deck and launched it over the side. Then they loaded the outboard and hooked it to the transom. Soon they were filling the fuel tank and dropping it into the dink as well.

"Ready?" Sluggo asked.

"Yeah, ready as I'll every be," Treb replied.

With that Sluggo lifted the port lazarette hatch and stooped over, grabbing a Pelican waterproof case that was buried there the whole trip. It was heavy, and he grunted a little as he worked it out of the lazarette. Once clear he hoisted it above the lifelines and handed it to Treb. Treb took it as if it didn't weigh a thing, and placed it carefully in the bow of the Dinghy.

Sluggo grabbed a mesh dive bag filled with dive gear and hoisted it to Treb as well. Then we reached into the lazarette one last time and pulled out a couple of aluminum 80 dive tanks. "Hope this is enough air" he said, and he closed the lazarette hatch and jumped into the dinghy with Treb. With all the gear, it was a tight fit.

Chapter 27

. . . .

It was just after dawn when Pizzaro woke from a fitful sleep in his cabin. For the briefest of moments he forgot where he was. He very much wanted a cold beer. He sat on the edge of his bunk for a second getting his bearings, and then reached over and took a cigarette out, lighting it. He knew the fuckhead captain would give him a ration of shit for smoking below decks, but he was pissed off, tired and hot. He needed a cigarette, and he needed a cold brew. He took a deep hit on the cigarette and stood uneasily. He hated boats, and this was one of the worst he'd been on. He stood for a couple seconds clearing his head, and then took a deep hit off the cigarette and butted it out on the edge of the table, putting it back into the pack. He had no idea how long he'd be stuck out here, and he might need it later.

He walked out of his cabin still wearing the pants he'd worn for the last four days. His t-shirt was crumpled from sleep, but it still looked clean in the mirror, so he was happy with it. He turned in the small hallway and made his way to the stairs that led to the galley. He held firmly to the handrails as he made his way up the companionway and into the galley. There were a couple of the crew sitting there sipping coffee. They were Filipino, and they said something that he didn't understand. He grumbled something at them that not even he understood, and reached into the refrigerator for a beer. It was a Hinano and he popped the top and turned it up in his mouth. As the cool and soothing elixir of life filled his mouth and throat he started to think he might actually make it through the day. He finished the beer off in two more long swigs and grabbed another, heading toward the salon. Time to let the captain know just who was in charge here.

The captain was standing on the aft rail looking out into the lagoon. "Okay, can we get started now?" Pizzaro asked, "or did you want to play tidily winks first?" he whined sarcastically.

Captain Mike turned and looked at the man. When he'd first met Pizzaro he was a little intimidated. He carried a lot of power and had cut through a lot of red tape getting the boat fueled and supplied as fast as he had. But after the past few days at sea, he was starting to think that the guy was more than a little whacked. But he was his superior, and after so many years chartering to the company, he couldn't take any chances.

"Yes sir," Mike replied. We are just about ready to make the first dive. Did you want to go down?"

Pizzaro looked at him with a look of disdain and took a long swig from his beer. "Do I look like I want to go down?" he asked in the same sarcastic whine. Then he answered his own question. "No fuckin' way. You and your crew can go down and get the stuff. I'll keep the beer company up here!"

Pizzaro sat back into a deck chair as the Captain headed into the salon. He gazed around the boat and tried to figure out why anyone would want to live in a hell hole like this. Nothing but sand and palm trees. No bars, no night life. "How fucking boring is that?" he asked, with no one in earshot.

He heard the crew starting to get their gear together. They started a pile of gear on the swimstep, and soon the tanks and BCs were there and ready. The crew went back into the boat to get their suits on.

Then he noticed a native boat starting to get closer to the boat. He glanced at the boat and saw that it was a native girl. He didn't care much for the natives. He preferred the working girls of Honolulu. He watched as this girl sailed past the boat. Then he started to wonder. She wasn't fishing. She just kind of watched the boat out of the corner of her eye.

As she sailed past for the second time he knew there was something wrong. His years of training started to take over. He slowly got up from the chair and made his way into the salon. Just as he entered the Captain was coming out of his cabin. Pizzaro grabbed him by the arm, turning him to look out the smoked window. "See that girl over there?" he indicated with a pointing finger.

"Yeah, so?" replied the captain.

"She's casing the boat," he said. "Watch her. She will sail past, and then turn and do it again."

The captain watched, and soon he could see the man was not paranoid. She was watching them.

"When she gets on the port side of the boat, opposite the dinghy, get two of your guys and jump in the dink. There's no way she can outrun our outboard. Get her and bring her back here," Pizzaro directed.

As soon as she sailed by the boat and the dink was hidden from her sight, three men jumped in the dinghy and the 50 horsepower outboard Honda hummed to life. It only took about 30 seconds for them to overtake her and pull her into the dink. They left the pram adrift and brought her back to the boat. As soon a she was aboard Pizzaro grabbed her arm and dragged her down below.

"Okay," he hissed, "why are you watching us? Who are you working for?"

She sat on the floor shaking, her eye's the size of saucers.

Pizzaro was looking forward to a little torture to take his mind off the boat ride. He picked up Milani as if she were just a little rag doll. "Okay honey," he hissed, "You and I are going to get better acquainted." With that he reached out and tore her pareo off. She tried to use her hands to cover her body. He stood and smiled at her, loving the feeling of power he got.

Slowly he walked over the settee and picked up a spool of 1/4" line. He smiled wickedly and reached out, grabbing her wrist. As soon as he had her wrist in his hand she turned into a wild woman. She dropped to the floor, grabbing his hand, pushing her knee into his shin and using his weight, pulled him over her, causing him to fall into the galley. In the time she had lived with Ron he had taught her the basics of Judo, and even though she was a mere 100 pounds, she fought like a wildcat.

The two crewmen heard the sound of Pizzaro hitting the deck and opened the door between the salon and the aft deck. They looked in and saw Pizzaro laying on his back, with a very attractive naked lady sitting on his chest punching him in the face. They started to enter and help him when they heard him laugh. Pizzaro laughing could be a very scary sound. They stopped in their tracks. "Go outside," they heard him say. "I'm going to enjoy myself a little with this one."

They watched as he picked her up and threw her down on the settee. Then he turned and glared at them. "Well," he said, "I'm waiting!" They both tripped over themselves as they closed the door and headed out onto the deck.

Meanwhile, Pizzaro took the line and grabbed her wrist, this time taking care to protect himself. He quickly tied her hands above her head, and then tied her legs, wide apart, to the base of the settee. Then he stood back and leered at her. "So, you want to play rough huh?" He smiled. "Cool, we can do that."

He reached into his pocket and took out his knife. He slowly opened the blade and locked it into place.

Milani stared at him with eye's wide open. "No!" she cried. "You cannot. I am pregnant!"

This made him grin even wider. "Some happy islander no doubt. Too bad he'll never meet the baby. I'll be the first to teach it to say mommy!"

"He's not a native. He is a great warrior, and he will kill you, just like he did the others that came!" she screamed at him.

That stopped him. She must be married to Ron Tess, the guy he'd been chasing for the past months. This was going to be better than he ever expected.

He walked over at placed his hand on her belly, smiling at her. "Well, the first thing we need to do is maybe give him a little twin. What do you think of that idea?" he grinned. "You think if I reach inside I can feel him?"

The look in his eye's frightened her even more than the words he was saying. She pulled at the ropes until they started to cut into her wrists, and kept pulling even harder.

He ran his hand down her stomach and his fingers started to explore her dark pubic area...

Chapter 28

Once ashore Dick and Ron made their way around the lagoon, staying in the underbrush. They were trying to get as close as possible to the salvage vessel. As they got close they camouflaged themselves as best they could and settled in to watch.

Meanwhile, Treb and Sluggo were motoring toward a small pass that wasn't too far from Maverick. It wasn't big enough for a boat to get through, but you could swim through easily enough.

They beached the dinghy just outside the pass and worked their way up the atoll until they were able to see Maverick through the underbrush.

"Piece of cake!" Sluggo said, estimating the distance between them and the boat.

Treb wasn't so sure. He was a good diver, but Sluggo lived in dive gear. He wasn't quite as sure of this plan, but it was all they had.

"Let's do it!" said Sluggo, and crawled back towards the dinghy. He started to unpack the tanks and other gear, gingerly setting aside the Pelican case.

Treb started getting his gear on too. Once the tanks were strapped on, they cleared the regulators and walked to the waters edge, easing their way in. "Don't use your air until you have to," Sluggo said, "and remember to swim easy to conserve your air."

With that he dog paddled through the pass toward the lagoon. Now it would all be up to timing. Treb checked his watch. They had about two minutes and thirty seconds. They'd cut it pretty close. He looked out at the boat and saw two figures climbing onto the swim step of Maverick. It was Dick and Ron.

Ron slowly looked over the transom and saw two crewmen standing in the salon, and signaled to Dick it was clear. They made their way onto the aft deck, and at just that moment the two men turned and came out, closing the sliding door to the salon. Just like when they were back in Nam, they each took an opponent and "equalized" him. It was silent, and it was fast. They slowly lowered the bodies to the deck and worked their way toward the entrance to the salon.

Ron got there first and stopped dead. He stood paralyzed as he watched Pizzaro open the blade to his knife and sit down next to Milani, who was tied to the settee. Dick came up beside him and looked in. Seeing what was happening he turned to Ron and saw that he was paralyzed.

Dick slammed open the door and had Pizzaro on the floor in a split second. Milani started to scream, and stopped mid scream. Her face was a mask of pure fear, then amazement, and happiness. She saw Ronnie standing in the doorway.

All of a sudden Ron came back to life. He stepped into the salon, and as he stepped over Dick and Pizzaro, he reached down and, almost as an afterthought, hit Pizzaro with an open hand hard across his nose. In that moment Pizzaro's life ended. The bone from his nose broke straight and clean, and entered the brain.

Ron picked up the knife Pizzaro had dropped, and quickly sliced away the line that tied Milani. She folded into his arms, and for a moment they were the only two people in the world.

About 50 feet from the boat Treb and Sluggo put in their regulators and started to dive. It was about 150 feet down. Treb knew they would be pushing the tables, but they had to get down there fast.

Sluggo started to pull ahead, and Treb

followed him trying to conserve his air. In no time Sluggo was at the entrance to the boat and going in. Treb reached the entrance and looked around. They were still the only ones down there. He hoped Dick and Ron were okay on Maverick.

They swam down into the sunken vessel and found the hold. It was badly burned, and it was hard to make sense out of what they saw. They searched, and then they saw the steel containers they sought. Sluggo attached a small explosive device to the containers and gave the thumbs up sign to Treb. They exited the wreck.

It was a short time later when they slowly surfaced, carefully timing their stops so as to avoid the bends. When they reached the surface they swam over to Maverick and climbed onto the swim step. A very unhappy ship's captain was sitting tied to a deck chair, and their friend Dick was sitting on the stern rail. "So how was the fishing?" he asked, smiling.

"Not bad," replied Sluggo, "but I thought maybe Ron would want to bring in the big one," and he held up the detonator.

"You may want to wait a couple minutes," Dick smiled. "He's busy right now, interrogating a local," and he pointed to the main salon door where they could see Ron holding Milani. He turned and saw them watching him through the glass doors.

"Hey, can't a guy get a little privacy?" he

asked.

Sluggo held up the detonator in his hand. "Well, we were going to give you the honors, but if you're too busy!" he laughed.

Ron helped Milani to her feet. She was wearing one of the crewmen's sweatshirts and it was about three sizes too big for her, but the shining look in her eyes made her the most beautiful woman any of them had ever seen. She walked carefully out the door. "Would you mind if I took care of this?" she asked, smiling.

A rumble was heard from below, as the chemical was instantly vaporized.

Chapter 29

The S/V *Lost Soul* was approaching the west end of Catalina under full sail. It was a beautiful, sunny afternoon, and the winds were blowing her gently towards her goal. If you didn't know better, you'd think the three men standing on her deck were just finishing a day sail around the island, instead of a month-long cruise from Fanning Island.

Treb was at the wheel, and he adjusted her course a little to starboard as they cleared the rocks on the west end. "You know Dick," he said to his friend who was sitting on the aft deck box, "maybe you should put a manager into the Academy for awhile. We need to go do some more exploring. This sail was far too short."

"Yeah," chimed in Sluggo. "Maybe I'll give them little one-footed squishies and squigglies a break and sail off with you!"

On the shore, a very old and very happy Bob Fox stood with two of the prettiest ladies on the beach, watching *Lost Soul* approach the anchorage at Two Harbors.

"Well Mia, what are you and Eva going to do now that your men are back?" he smiled. "Things may be a little too tame for you now."

They moved up, one on each side, and leaned on him from both sides. "What's the matter Bob?" Mia asked. "We too much for you?"

An older lady just passing them on the pier looked at them with disgust as she passed. "Well, I never heard of such a thing," She said to her husband.

Her husband just shook his head and said under his breath, "Yeah, I know!"

Epilog

Ron was sitting on the edge of his bed, looking at Milani holding their new son. Ione was just finishing the naming ceremony. When a new member is born into society it is a big event for the whole community, as there is no doubt, in the ensuing years everyone's life affects the others. He thought of the old poem by John Donne, "No Man is an Island," and smiled. It was even more true in an island society.

The other villagers weren't too sure about the name. Somehow, "Dick" just didn't fit the Polynesian tongue, but he was a beautiful and healthy baby boy.

For the first time in his life, Ron knew he was home.

About The Author

Robert "Bob Bitchin" Lipkin was born in Los Angeles, California in 1944. He spent 28 years riding motorcycles around the United States and Europe, writing of his experiences in all of the major motorcycles magazines of the '70s and '80s.

In the early '70s he acted as roustabout and bodyguard for famous motorcycle daredevil Evil Knievel, and later produced "CycleExpo," one of the largest motorcycle shows on the West Coast. During most of those years he lived aboard various sailboats that he would buy in rundown condition and restore to sell.

He went on to create *BIKER NEWS, BIKER Magazine and TATTOO Magazine*. In the mid '80s he sold his magazines and retired.

He spent several years sailing the Pacific, first on his Formosa 51' ketch *Lost Soul*, and then on an aft-cockpit Formosa 51 named *Predator*. In 1991 he purchased a derelict 68' ketch, which he renamed *Lost Soul*. A year later, after extensive repairs, he departed with his ladyfriend Jody on a voyage that would take them to the four corners of the globe.

Five years later they returned, and he founded *LATITUDES & ATTITUDES Magazine*, which has gone on to become the largest magazine in its field. He also created the weekly TV show *Latitudes & Attitudes* with his friend Darren O'Brien. He now spends his time between Redondo Beach, sailing, and his home in the Sierra Nevada mountains, in Berry Creek, California.

Other books of interest From Bob Bitchin
· ·

A Brotherhood of Outlaws
The first Treb Lincoln novel. See what the life
of an outlaw biker was really like in the '70s.
Learn about the brotherhood and the feeling of
comeraderie and what it was like riding in the
heyday of the American outlaw biker. True to life!

Letters from the Lost Soul
The true story of a five year voyage all over the
world. Travel with Bob Bitchin and his wife
Jody aboard the 60' ketch *Lost Soul* from the sun
drenched beaches of Bora Bora to the Islands of
Greece and the beautiful Caribbean.

The Sailing Life
A collection of insights into the world of cruising,
as seen by the founder and publisher of Latitudes
& Attitudes Magazine and the television show of
the same name. See what makes people love the
cruising lifestyle.

Emerald Bay
This novel follows Treb Lincoln as he tries to learn
what caused the death of his young wife in a boating
explosion in peaceful Emerald Bay. The trail leads to
places you would least expect. Fast paced.

BIKER
A collection of true stories showing just what kind
of fun and games a man can get into when he rides
the highways of America. These are true stories
that will keep you asking yourself: "Now who the
hell would done something like that?!"

All these titles are available at:
www.seafaring.com   888-8-WE-SAIL